M000300401

Cajun Zombie Chronicles:
Book One

THE
RIVER DEAD

by

S. L. Smith

HOLY WATER BOOKS

BROADCAST TRANSCRIPT b:23:10:36

\>> What were once thought to be riots ... food shortages ... [GARBLED]

\>> Beginning in urban areas [STATIC] reports of erratic behavior, cannibalism ...

\>> Monsanto spokesperson claims no connection ... not liable for effects ... [STATIC]

\>> [STATIC] ... Shelters compromised ... [GARBLED]

\>> Reports of the dead rising ...

\>> ... Containment efforts failing ...

END TRANSMISSION

Cajun Zombie Chronicles: Book One
The River Dead

ISBN-13: 978-1-950782-06-2 (Holy Water Books)

HOLY WATER BOOKS
At the unexpected horizons of the New Evangelization

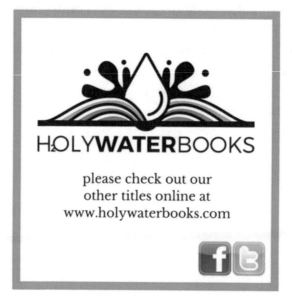

HOLYWATERBOOKS

please check out our
other titles online at
www.holywaterbooks.com

Cover design by Holy Water Books

Cajun Zombie Chronicles: Book One
THE RIVER DEAD

Table of Contents

CHAPTER ONE: THE CUT MEN 1

CHAPTER TWO: SANCTUARY..................... 11

CHAPTER THREE: THE FENCE.................... 20

CHAPTER FOUR: THE RECTORY........................... 28

CHAPTER FIVE: MORNING 35

CHAPTER SIX: THE SNAKE............................ 46

CHAPTER SEVEN: THE APPROACH.................... 54

CHAPTER EIGHT: THE BRIDGE 60

CHAPTER NINE: STARTER RAIDS 69

CHAPTER TEN: NO FREE MEALS 77

CHAPTER ELEVEN: WAL-MARTIANS.................... 82

CHAPTER TWELVE: NEW GREEN 96

CHAPTER THIRTEEN: INDEFECTABILITY.................... 102

CHAPTER FOURTEEN: COUNTDOWN 106

CHAPTER FIFTEEN: UNION.................................... 112

CHAPTER SIXTEEN: CARDINALS FANS........................ 119

CHAPTER SEVENTEEN: BIRNAM WOOD...................... 125

CHAPTER EIGHTEEN: BOXED-OFF 133

CHAPTER NINETEEN: THE ABBOT'S VISION.............. 138

CHAPTER TWENTY: HERD 146

CHAPTER TWENTY-ONE: PADRE...................................... 153

CHAPTER TWENTY-TWO: COWS AND CODDLING ... 163

CHAPTER TWENTY-THREE: COJONES 169

CHAPTER TWENTY-FOUR: ....
BOWLING ALLEY CHURCHES................................ 175

CHAPTER TWENTY-FIVE: RADIO....................................... 179

EPILOGUE: THE INTERSTATE... 183

READ THE SEQUELS NEXT... 190

CHAPTER ONE:
THE CUT MEN

"Sara." He took his wife's delicate face into his hands. "You've got to help me keep the kids quiet."

"Ma-daddy, I wanna watch a *show!*" The little girl kept tugging at the man's belt. Her little hands kept prying at the snap of his pistol holster. The man looked around nervously and left abruptly to make one last sweep of their house.

"Emma Claire," Sara said, lowering herself to her knees and putting her face close to her daughter's. She took the girl's soft face into her hands, and spoke softly but firmly. "Emma Claire, look at me in my eyes. There are no more shows. The TV stopped working last week, remember?" The little girl nodded her head distractedly, trying to see where her daddy had gone. "You're going to be *quiet* now. For your daddy, right? Say, yes, ma'am."

"Yes, ma-mommy." The girl said sweetly beneath a mop of sweaty curls. Even as she did, her baby brother cooed from inside the pack strapped to her mother's chest.

"Dee-dee stay ky-it, too! Sshh!" The little girl instructed her little brother in imitation of her mother.

"You're gonna stay quiet, Emma, because if you don't, something bad could happen to us. Do you understand?"

"The cut men," the little girl replied. "Elmole come, too?"

"No," the father said with a wry smile, overhearing the conversation from another part of the house. "Elmole isn't coming."

Sara turned her daughter's head back to her. "Yes, that's right. The cut men. They're out there and they can hear us. If you say anything, they can hear you. If they hear you, they may take you away from mommy and daddy. And – and you'll never see us again. Do you understand?"

Giant tears formed at the girl's eyes, and she nodded. "I stay ky-it," she choked out.

"Okay, mi familia." The man returned. Though his eyes glistened with fresh tears, a smile creased his face. "Everybody get it in the car. Sara, I'll snap the kids in their child seats, like we planned."

"And I'll cover you all from the porch with my bow," Sara answered. She had grown up with firearms, hunting with her family, while her husband was a relative novice. He was fine with the basics – pistols, rifles, and shotguns – but hadn't yet mastered the quieter implements, like a compound bow, which was much more useful in their current situation.

"Be careful, Smithy." She smiled at her husband and kissed him, but her hands were trembling.

"Okay. Come here, little guy." The man unsnapped the baby boy from his mother's pack. The baby gurgled quietly and tensed up briefly, stretching. Smithy, as his wife called him, tucked the boy's head under his chin and braced himself. The man's name was actually Isherwood Smith, which was why Sara chose to call her husband by variants of his *last* name.

They had no garage, so they would be basically sitting ducks if more than one or two of those "cut men" shambled by. The back trunk space of their Honda CR-V was meticulously packed. Isherwood had snuck out into the relative safety of the darkness the night before to prepare for their forced evacuation. He cursed himself for waiting so long to upgrade the family vehicle. They were forced to leave some of their canned goods and other supplies behind due to limited space. Isherwood had not yet fully accepted the change that had come over the world. He still refused to steal a vehicle, though he was quickly warming to the idea.

"It's okay, Smith." Sara had insisted. "The smaller vehicle will help on gas." His wife had been mostly serene throughout the whole unfolding of chaos. He had been subconsciously leaning on her steadfastness. That's where he'd found his courage these past several days.

Isherwood knew that his wife was bottling up, if only for her husband's sanity, her worries about her own family, with the exception of her aunt and uncle who lived across the street. She was still checking her phone for a message from her mom or dad or one of her brothers and sisters. The phone had likely stopped working days ago, but she still held out hope that a blip of electricity could restore the networks just long enough for a text message to be delivered to her. The last she heard, they were all heading to their camp at Whiskey Bay. Whiskey Bay was located in the Atchafalaya River Basin, which was mostly lakes and swamp. Though off the grid, it was right along Interstate 10. The camp was midway between Lafayette and Baton Rouge. The interstate through there, Isherwood believed, was likely packed with cars, as that section of the interstate was nearly all bridges for twenty or thirty miles. The Whiskey Bay exit ramp had likely become a primary artery of zombies leaving the raised roadway. Nevertheless, if the zombies weren't spilling over the sides of the interstate into the swamp twenty-five feet below, Sara's family might have found refuge on the island portion of Whiskey Bay. The "Island," as they called it, was bound on either side by the Atchafalaya River and the man-made Pilot Channel until the point where they re-converged. There were no exit ramps leading from the interstate onto the Island.

But Isherwood stuffed all this to the back of his mind, as they were in no state whatsoever to make the long trip to Whiskey Bay. That would have to wait until they established some kind of long-term shelter right here in St. Maryville.

They had attempted to shelter in place on Delaware Avenue, as Isherwood's grandmother and aunt, as well as Sara's aunt and uncle, all lived right across the street. Instead of bugging out immediately when the tide had turned irrevocably in favor of "the cut men," they had bugged in.

Their collective supplies had been sufficient for this first week, but were quickly dwindling. They were not serious preppers, but they had enjoyed watching the reality shows. They had half-heartedly incorporated some strategies, but all those had been subsumed into their attempts at homesteading. And now, their backyard chickens and ducks were nothing but a zombie swarm magnet. Isherwood had been forced to release most of the animals. He had bitterly regretted getting rid of their food source, but Sara had had an alternate plan.

*****

Several days earlier …

"I can't believe that crappy pallet fence I built is holding up."

"Smith, look!" Sara was nudging her husband hard as they attempted to peak into their own backyard through the blinds.

"*Shhh*," Isherwood grumbled. "They're gonna *hear* us. And then that sick moaning will start again."

"Sorry!" she whispered. "I just got a little excited." They were kneeling down in the back room of their house, which had only days before served as the nursery. They were watching the ongoing struggle between the zombies and their chickens. Their chicken pen had been slowly attracting a lot of undesired notice. "Look down at the bottom, towards the ground. You see Henny's little head?"

"Man, my eyes suck. I can't hardly – wait. Is she? What's she doing?"

"She's nibbling on him!"

"She's what?"

"That little boy zombie with the shorts – Henny's pecking at his legs."

4

"Good God, they'll eat *anything*." As Isherwood's eyes focused, he could just make out twin patches of missing flesh on the boy's uncovered legs. Being just a little taller than the pallets, there was no risk that the boy would tumble over head first into their small chicken yard. It was the taller zombies – there were just a couple, thankfully – that could be trouble.

"Do you get what this could mean?" Sara was nudging her husband's arm again.

"Yeah, chicken zombies!" Isherwood whispered back in irritation.

"Maybe. Maybe *not*." She smiled mischievously. "It might mean we get to kill two birds with one stone … and dine on fat birds."

"Always with the extended idioms. What're you talking about? All I see is yet another way we're losing the chickens."

"Just you wait. I'm gonna use Honey's old cage. It's not like we have any use for it anymore." Honey *had* been their backyard guard dog. She had always been a little too friendly for her duties, but she had kept intruders out well enough. That was until zombies started showing up. Her incessant barking was drawing in a frightening amount of zombies. Even still, Isherwood had hesitated to kill her, and was preparing to bring her inside over Sara's sharp admonitions. A sharp yelp from the old dog, and Isherwood knew the argument was over. The zombies had ploughed through their somewhat rickety garden gate to get to the dog. The dog had been swarmed, and the zombies had had free reign of the yard ever since.

"Use Honey's cage? For what?" Isherwood asked, though his whispers were hardly carrying the distance to his wife anymore.

"*You'll* see." Sara smiled and winked after he had caught up with her. "We're gonna draw those suckers away from our house *and* keep the chickens fed."

"You're gonna get my chickens killed, that's what's gonna happen."

"Well," Sara paused, thinking. "You'll probably hafta be our guinea pig, taste-testing the eggs in case they turn us all into zombies."

"What! *What* are you talking about?"

"Here, Ish, go kill those things out there, will ya?" Sara said, handing her husband a pillow. Their supplies of pillows were quickly dwindling. Isherwood had been stockpiling 9mm ammunition for a year or more, but he had never thought to buy a silencer for his pistol. "I'll cover you with the bow from the window."

Isherwood was just standing there stubbornly. "Look," Sara said, "you need to go kill those things anyway, don't you? I'll explain everything when you get back. We'll get Henny and Penny and the rest in the cage when you get back.

Isherwood, despite having been a seat warmer at a desk job his entire adult life, had grown adept at killing zombies with surprising speed. A mixture of hunting with his in-laws and a consistent diet of zombie movies, comics, and books had probably helped. He was also smart. He had graduated as a chemical engineer, but had switched from one field of engineering to another a couple times. Generally, though, his employers had kept him behind a desk optimizing their operations. "Optimizing, always optimizing," as his wife was often heard grumbling to herself.

Isherwood moved quickly through his back yard, scanning along sight lines and keeping tight against cover. Though he would never admit it, he was just doing his best impression of television agents and operatives. But it worked.

Sara watched as her husband approached the first zombie. *This weirdo's just staring at my shed*, she thought, as she watched the zombie just wobble back and forth nowhere near the chickens.

Isherwood quickly pushed the plaid pillow, which had so long adorned their couch, and his 9mm against the back of the creature's head. He fired a single, muffled shot. After working so hard to stockpile the ammunition, he hated wasting shots. The zombies' skulls had not yet softened with rot. An ill-aimed knife plunge would still glance right off the skull, slicing off an ear or scalping the already ugly things.

Nevertheless, Isherwood avoided the double-tap that had been advised in the movies. When he would finish clearing out the backyard, he would just do a once-over with a sledge hammer. One good thrust down, as with a post-hole digger or a broad sword, was usually enough to flatten the skull.

Soon enough, he had made his way past the compost bins and was taking care of business around the perimeter of the chicken coop. There were four altogether, not counting Sara's "weirdo" staring at the shed. But that was not all. Isherwood heard the crunch of grass behind him. He knew with a sickening feeling in his gut that he was too late. He turned in time to see the zombie's wide open and drooling mouth come lunging toward him. Their spines had a way of arching backward like a viper and snapping forward just before the first bite.

Before he could even raise his arm in an instinctual move of protection, Isherwood felt the spray of half-coagulated blood splatter across his face. The zombie's head and torso seized up mid-lunge as his wife's arrow sliced straight through its skull. The broadhead of the arrow lodged into a cypress tree across the chicken yard with a *thunk!*

Isherwood spat out the black sludge that had splashed into his open mouth. "*Ugh!* Feels like cheese curds." Luckily, the yard was now free of zombies, as Isherwood was all consumed with disgust.

"What?" He whispered back in the direction of the house.

"No kissing me tonight, Smithy." His wife called back a little louder.

"Nice shot, hun." He called back. Moments later, his wife came trudging through the back yard struggling to carry their dead dog's oversized and unwieldy kennel.

"Help me load 'em up in here." She instructed her husband. "Come on. Just trust me."

When she noticed that her husband had finally relented in helping her with her half-explained plan for the chickens, she slipped over to the cypress tree to reclaim her arrow. She was equally miserly with her arrows as Isherwood was with his bullets. She wiggled it back and forth, careful not to apply too much pressure to where the shaft met the spine.

After returning the arrow to her quiver, she retrieved Penny from her perch atop the neighbor's fence. There was a brief thrashing of wings and clucking as she spooked the chicken, but Sara tucked the bird under her arm and it quickly quieted.

"Okay, now what?" Isherwood asked after stuffing Penny into the cage.

"*Now,* I need you to carry that cage out across the street – I'll cover you from the porch. Put it near a puddle or in a ditch, so they'll have access to water. Food's not gonna be an issue."

"How 'bout the front yard of the Braud sisters' house?" Isherwood smiled vengefully. He had long hated the sight of the blighted property at the end of their street. He had admitted to Sara that demolishing that old rat trap was top on his post-apocalypse bucket list.

"That's fine. Better there than in the road in case we want to use bungee sticks at some point."

"Use what? You mean *punji* sticks?"

"Yeah, that's what I said. 'Punji.'" She smiled sheepishly.

"Suuure, you did."

They returned smiles at each other. Sara more so, because she knew she had Isherwood in the right frame of mind now to carry out her idea. She knew he could do pretty much whatever he wanted – or whatever *she* wanted – if she could just get him to stumble into the right mood.

"You know," he nodded, approvingly. "This might just work. The cage is good because they can peck out of it, but the zombies won't be able to get their whole hands in. Just so long as the weight of all those bodies doesn't collapse the cage."

They found a new source of entertainment that afternoon watching the scattered zombies on their street stagger over to the noisy cage of chickens. The zombies congregated there, cleaning up their end of Delaware Avenue. It also made it easy for Isherwood to move around the perimeter, picking off the zombies one by one, as they groped, utterly entranced, at the cage.

"It works so well – I don't even think we need the bungee sticks," Isherwood said, nudging his wife with a sly smile.

*****

But that had all happened in the first couple days of the crisis, while the zombies were all still, for the most part, locals. There hadn't been many locals.

In the meantime, the dreams had started. Isherwood couldn't tell by the light of day what were his ideas and what were flashes of his dreams. It didn't matter, though. A plan had formed.

As Sara scanned the street, she half-noticed the still-functioning chicken trap on the other end of the street. It had turned into a massive hill of zombies, like a slowly-putrefying Indian burial mound. Isherwood hadn't bothered to remove the bodies. The pressure of zombies stacking on top of zombies had provided the chickens, not only with a food source inside their surprisingly sturdy cage, but with a water source, as well. Sara grimaced, and a chill vibrated down her spine, as she thought about what Henny, Penny, and the rest's diet must now consist of.

Luckily, the increased numbers of zombies ambling down Delaware Avenue didn't notice the Smith family until the last buckle of the last car seat clicked into place. But it didn't matter.

At the sound of the last click, Sara, too, moved into action. She slid the little black button on the butt of Emma Claire's annoying furry red "Tickle Me Elmo" toy into the "on" position. She hurled it into the road like a hand grenade. As it landed, the toy started jostling back and forth on the asphalt as the tickle mechanism began vibrating. Then, the toy's little voice started echoing across the deathly stillness of the street. It did its job perfectly. Every zombie up and down the street, even those still trying to scramble up "Mount Zombie" to get at the chickens, turned towards the toy.

At the sound of it and nearly simultaneously, the engines of a truck and another, newer CRV roared to life across the street. It was Sara's Aunt Tad and Uncle Jerry in the truck. They lived right across the street from the Smiths. And, two houses down, in the driveway of the great house Isherwood's great-grandfather had built, his grandmother and aunt starting inching backward towards the road.

In a flash, Sara was in the CRV. Isherwood was behind the wheel and already holding the button down to open the car's sun roof. Sara slid the compound bow across the length of the black plastic dashboard, and took a pistol from Isherwood's outstretched hand.

"Whoa, mommy!" Emma clapped, as Sara pulled herself up through the sun roof to stand there as the human turret of their improvised tank.

"You remember to get down if it gets too bouncy, okay?" Isherwood nervously reminded his wife.

"Got it, babe." She said, checking the clip and snapping it back into place. As she did it, Isherwood noticed that her hands were no longer trembling.

The CRV slid out from the driveway and the two other vehicles slipped into line behind it. They let Isherwood's grandmother and aunt drive in the safer, middle position of their caravan. Aunt Tad leveled a shotgun out of her passenger window as Uncle Jerry drove the truck at the end of their line.

CHAPTER TWO: SANCTUARY

Even when their situation had seemed more tenable, Isherwood and Sara had been planning, along with their relatives along Delaware Avenue, to move to a safer location. "What we really need is a *castle!*" Several nights ago, Sara and Isherwood had been whispering together, killing time before their shifts began for the night watch.

Isherwood had laughed and then wondered aloud at the suggestion, "A castle?" A memory of a dream flashed through his mind.

"Yeah, you got one of those stashed away?"

"Well – but you're right, you know. Castles were made to survive a prolonged siege, and that, one day, is probably coming. We may not have Windsor Castle in St. Maryville, but we do have some options. The Edward Jones building is solid brick."

"Yeah, there's the Parish Jail, too. Or even *Angola,*" Sara suggested.

"You're right. We'd probably have to clean those places out. Angola might be packed with eight thousand zombies in stripes and ankle irons. But, they'd have plenty of enclosed space for farming, orchards, …"

"Even ranching," Sara added.

"They're sort of like modern castles, but ... but what if? ... hey now, I think I've got something. There's a gothic castle of sorts just a couple blocks from here. Thick doors, solid brick, high windows, lots of enclosed land, multiple buildings, kitchens – can you guess?" Isherwood's eyes gleamed as he turned to his wife with his little riddle. He laughed as she muddled her face in confusion.

"The *church*, of course," Isherwood grabbed his wife by her shoulders and shook her.

"The what?"

"It needs protection from those things, too. They'll just desecrate the whole thing."

"But we can't just –"

"Oh no!" Isherwood's face went suddenly pale. "Do you think Monsignor's still alive in there? Oh Jeez! I don't think I could kill his zombie. But what if he's alive? He could've probably used our help a long time ago."

"Calm down, Smithy," Sara had shrugged off her own confusion as she watched her husband's confusion fester. "We'll get to that soon enough. It really is a great idea. There's probably five or six acres inside the fences."

"Yeah, and the river would be at our backs, cutting off the directions we could be swarmed from."

"And the river means fresh water and fish – you know, I bet there's an old well on the church grounds, too." Sara was nodding vigorously now. Her little spiral notebook – her "Idea Book," as she called it – had even appeared in her hands.

"The main church building would be like the strong room of the castle, the castle keep. It would be ..."

"... Sanctuary," Sara smiled.

*****

The caravan of vehicles turned west onto Fifth Street, turning left out of Delaware Avenue. The dead turned slowly in the direction of the passing cars. They began stumbling towards the cars just as they disappeared from view. They then began following in the direction of their fading engines.

Isherwood had planned to drive along the narrower side streets to avoid any large groups of zombies, but they would still need to cross Maryville Street. Only a block from their homes, they passed along the southern edge of the town cemetery. It was several acres of marble and granite vaults, like a scale model of the city of Rome. Ironically, there were relatively few dead shambling through the graveyard. Even the dead, it seemed, respected the dead.

It was a short drive through downtown St. Maryville to reach their new location, but none of the others, besides Isherwood, had yet witnessed the devastation beyond Delaware Avenue. Isherwood had gone on several scavenging runs down to the grocery store at the other end of Delaware Avenue, but even he had not ventured far from home, not wanting to leave his wife and babies alone for long.

They were all struck by the patches where the destruction had been most severe: the burned out hulks of an old Victorian home and several crashed vehicles. There were several looted store fronts. A telephone pole had collapsed across Maryville Street. Smoke was still rising from Maggio Oldsmobile, one of only two car dealerships in town. Even despite obvious signs of burglary, the car lot was still full of seemingly untouched rows of vehicles. Isherwood was eyeing the trucks as they passed by. It was a Jeep, though, that he had always wanted, but he had always needed something more family-friendly.

"Whoa!" Sara yelled as their CRV suddenly bounced into the air and something soft scuffled under the vehicle. "Watch out, Smith. If that thing had bounced onto the hood it might be chewing on your ear right now."

"You're the only one that gets to chew on my ear," Isherwood said, attempting to cover up his momentary loss of focus. He hadn't even seen the zombie that he had hit. As his attention returned to the road, he began to notice that the dead were pretty evenly spaced around the buildings and in the roads. There were no denser pockets. It looked like they had spread out purposefully, as part of some kind of predatory behavior, like a dragnet. As he checked behind their caravan, he noticed that the zombies that had started following them were starting to coalesce into larger groups.

"What are you doing now? This isn't the way." Sara observed from her perch. They were passing by a surveying company and the newspaper building. The streets were studded here and there with abandoned vehicles, but less so on the side streets. It was as Isherwood had planned, but the side streets could get narrow in a hurry.

"Make a circling motion with your hand to tell the others that I'm taking us around a couple extra blocks to lose our tail. And check out the church and especially those gates as we pass by, okie dokie?" Isherwood was trying his best to keep his voice even, but the panic was beginning to feel like a fist rising up his throat.

"Maybe you should drop me off now, so I can have the gates ready to open when you pass back through?"

"No, Sara. I'm not risking it. We'll make one more pass. Who knows? Maybe we'll even have a welcoming party next time around, a *live* one."

They skirted the edge of the church property and headed back north up Poydras Avenue, then turned west on Seventh Street to avoid the clustering dead they may have provoked on Fifth Street. They looped back south again passing by the local high school and elementary. On the far side of the school, Isherwood noted for future reference, was the local library.

Both schools were surrounded by chain link fences and gates. It was a sturdy enclosure, though not as sturdy as the church's old wrought-iron fence. The church fence had even been reinforced over the years. It was also tall. Taller than he was, Isherwood knew that much. It may even be seven or eight feet. Not only was it tall, each rod of the fence was capped either with a spear point or the more decorative fleur-de-lis at intervals.

"All the gates I saw were padlocked, Smith." Sara informed her husband.

"That's what I saw, too," he grimaced. "Looks like St. Christopher's gonna hafta bail us out of this one."

14

They were now driving along the northern fence line of the church. Another hundred yards or so, and they'd be at their entrance.

"What're we worrying about? We can just leave the cars parked outside and get ourselves in for now – come back for our cars once the crowds scatter."

"What?" Sara said, dismayed. "What're you thinking? We're just gonna toss our babies over that fence? Even if we could get the babies over, what's your Gran gonna do?"

Isherwood looked crestfallen. "We'll just have to bug *way* out of town and come back. But, who knows what could happen? We may never get another chance at this, Sara."

"There's the gate again," Sara said quietly. They could both see that nothing had changed. No one had appeared to help them, and something even worse had happened.

"Well," Isherwood said, his voice staring to shake. "Looks like a welcoming party showed up after all." All their driving around had apparently stirred up the hornet's nest. Instead of the zombies being spread out and aimless, there were groups of zombies *and* they were converging on them from all sides.

"Crap," Sara said, no longer whispering. She took in the full three hundred sixty degree view, stepping back and forth on the cloth seats of the CRV. "We gotta get that thing open."

"We gotta go, Sara. *Now*, while we still can." Isherwood tried pulling her down into the seat. Just then, they jumped as the car windows rattled. It was Aunt Tad with her shotgun, firing the first salvo.

"Smith!" Sara suddenly called out. "Did you see that?"

"See what?"

"Something just peaked at us from the far side of that shed. Take *this*, Smithy. Give me cover. We're getting in *right now*." She pushed his 9mm back into his hands, and then, sitting on the roof of the car, swung her legs out. Isherwood next saw the blur of her butt as she slid down the windshield and bounded off the hood.

"Your bow!" Isherwood called to her, putting the CRV in park and closing the driver side door behind him. "At least take your …"

15

"Watch out, Ish!" Isherwood spun on his heels as his aunt called to him from inside the second vehicle. The first pack was almost on him, but he was looking around for a pillow to silence the shots.

"Screw it," Isherwood said to himself. "Come on cue ball." He walked right up to the first zombie, and, taking it by the neck, shoved its head into the one behind it. He put his pistol to the first skull and fired. The heads clacked together like billiard balls and then exploded.

Sara could hear her husband going to work behind her. She grabbed the bars of the gate and shouted, "Get over here and help us!"

The smallish shadow again came peeping around the far side of the shed. "Tattoo! I can see you! Get your butt and your keys *over here.*" She growled the last words, using a register of her voice only accessible to mothers.

Shamefaced, a short man stepped into the light. He was just standing there fumbling in his pockets, trying not to look at Sara. "GET YOUR BUTT OVER HERE, TATTOO!" Sara said rattling the iron bars of the gate, every bit the mother bear protecting her children.

The little man scurried over to the gate. His feet and legs seemed to know what they were doing before the rest of him did. The keys kept slipping from the man's small plumpish hands. After two failed attempts at opening the gate, Sara took the keys. The man shrunk in size as though the keys were the single most significant part of his personality. He faded backward slowly, turning his focus toward the oncoming calamity.

Isherwood was moving quickly through the oncoming zombies, darting from pack to pack. He was counting rounds. He didn't remember if he had pressed that extra sixteenth bullet in both his magazine and backup magazine. The last thing he wanted to hear was that terrible empty clicking sound of being out of ammo as one of those things began to wrap its fingers around his throat or worse, get a nip of his clothes. After the thirteenth round, he was about to dart into the midst of a pack of three zombies. He was now clear across the road and ditch that ran along the back of the church. The next pack of zombies had just stumbled through a line of privet bushes which marked the edge of a parking lot the church shared with a Masonic Lodge.

As Isherwood darted over to the still-stumbling zombies, he realized the group coming through the privets was still growing. "The packs are growing!" Isherwood called, turning back to Sara and the caravan, but his voice was drowned out by the *ka-blam* of Uncle Jerry's shotgun.

Isherwood cursed before he could bite his lip closed. Uncle Jerry's shotgun blast had knocked the head off one of the nearest zombies. The next two in line had staggered backward, as well. The spray of steel shot had also nicked Isherwood. He fought back the instinct to rub his calf in pain. "Watch your choke on that thing!" Isherwood grunted, as he tapped the button on the grip of his pistol to switch out magazines. He took out the next five or so that were scrambling through the bushes, and was forced to begin retreating backward, as a near-solid line of fifteen ghouls staggered through the line of bushes all at once.

Luckily, Sara and Isherwood both knew the church and the gates well. It was one of the main reasons why they had eventually decided to go through with this plan. Sara had found the key she needed after grabbing the over-sized key ring from Tattoo, but it was tricky work. She was working blind and backward, reaching through the bars of the gate to turn the key in the padlock. She heard a satisfying *click* inside the Master-Lock and exhaled the breath she hadn't realized she'd been holding.

Isherwood had retreated from the bushes along the Masonic Lodge and was busy knocking out two smaller packs that were staggering toward them from Main Street. He was careful to guide the falling bodies into the ditches on either side of the road. Otherwise, the growing piles might block the caravan's only escape route. As he looked up from dropping a middle-aged woman zombie – once a Districts Bank teller, he thought – Isherwood saw that two gangs of zombies further along the road were the thickest mobs yet. They were staggering nearly perfectly abreast, filling the entire width of the road, like a brigade of gray confederate soldiers.

Just as Isherwood was about to call out a warning, he heard the blessed sound of the iron gate's old brass wheels creaking along their tracks. He looked back to see Sara smiling at him broadly, as she pushed the gate open with her shoulder.

"Get in the CRV. I'll cover you," Isherwood called to her. He was free to retreat backward into the safe zone he had created, even as solid lines of the dead approached from two out of the three remaining directions. At his back, he heard Sara slam the door and shift the CRV out of park. He thought he might have heard his little girl start crying for him, as his little family ark rumbled across the tracks of the gate into the quiet and safety of the church parking lot beyond. The second CRV and Uncle Jerry's truck were quick to follow.

In his excitement, Isherwood had lost track of the spent rounds in his second and last magazine. It was either twelve or lucky number thirteen again. It didn't really matter. He would need another whole magazine to take out even one of the mobs coming at him.

The line of zombies approaching from the Masonic Lodge were nearer than the confederate horde approaching from Main Street. He called to them, "Hey, over *here*. Can't you jerks walk straight?"

He was calling to them from the turn in the roadway. Isherwood had seen in a flash that he would be home free if he could just guide the line into the ditch lining the roadway. They would eventually mound up creating their own bridge, but it would take time. True to form, the dead responded to Isherwood's insults, and he began retreating towards the gate.

A thought flashed across his mind. He sure hoped they were covering his back, because he had lost any awareness momentarily of what stood between him and the gate. *It was still clear ... wasn't it?*

Isherwood spun around to see an unwelcome face and snapping jaws.

Thwack!

The thing's head lurched to one side as a rifle shot cracked in one side of its skull and exploded through the other half. Bits of rotted brain and skull fragments sprayed across the road, even as the zombie was thrown down by the force of the impact, almost somersaulting sideways.

The next sound Isherwood heard was the creaking of the gate's brass wheels along their track. "Get in here, buster," he heard his Gran call to him. "That was too close." In another moment, he was watching the faces of the dead press in harmlessly against the iron fence. The fence stood solid. The rotting arms were reaching for them through the bars, groping desperately at empty air.

CHAPTER THREE:
THE FENCE

Isherwood was just standing there holding his wife. He had tucked his wife's head under his chin and was holding her as they both caught their breaths. He listened as the swarms of zombies hit the fence. The fence groaned as each group slammed against it.

Aunt Tad and the other women ran back to the fences with their weapons. Lizzy and Isherwood's grandmother, Mrs. Lorio, still weren't comfortable using knives. They had instead used their knives to sharpen the ends of broomsticks. Lizzy and Mrs. Lorio were also shorter than most all the zombies. Instead of stabbing through the fence at the zombies' temples, like Tad, they plunged their broomsticks up and through the underside of the jaw bone. They had each already practiced this motion several times protecting their home during the last week. For petite women, they found they wielded quite a bit of force with this upward thrusting motion.

Mrs. Lorio winced as she stabbed her broomstick handle up through the bearded neck of an older man. He had been trying to squeeze his thick head through the iron bars of the fence. He had been pushing with such ferocity that he had sheared off his ears and cheeks in the process.

There was a popping sound as the head became unstuck as it was launched backward. "Oh, dear," she said as she yanked the shaft back out. "He used to be my air conditioner repair man."

"Wow," Aunt Lizzy smirked. "He's nothing but a pile of goo now."

"Come on, Ish." Uncle Jerry tapped Isherwood on the shoulder. "Let's check out the rest of the fence before we get too cozy."

Isherwood groaned, finally pulling away from his wife. "You're right. This could all come tumbling down on us if that fence isn't solid."

"Wait," Sara growled. "What about your leg? Remember how you shot my husband, Uncle?"

"Just a little stinger." Jerry smiled. "But where'd that rifle shot come from?"

"Don't know, but must be one of the good guys, right? Hope we find out soon. An extra hand and a good shot, too, would be nice." As he said it, he was feeling around his calf muscle and trying to look through the new hole in his jeans. "Yeah Sara, he's right. No immediate need. I can walk on it fine. After you've dispatched these twenty or so, get everybody inside or at least inside the rectory's fence for now. We don't want to draw any extra attention just yet. Maybe we'll get lucky and Monsignor will still be here and alive. We'll sweep the perimeter for holes, come back, and start sweeping buildings."

Isherwood nodded at Sara and the rest, and was about to turn and run off to walk the fence line.

Sara grabbed his shoulder, jolting him backward. "Ah," Isherwood smiled. "A parting kiss for your husband, the hero?"

"Sort of," Sara said, tapping the firearm Isherwood was still holding. "You need to reload."

"Oh, yeah." Isherwood nodded, as his cheeks registered crimson. Isherwood left the little group of ladies and Uncle Jerry to reload from the box of rounds he had left in the front seat of the CRV.

"Going to church, ma-daddy?" Emma called from the back seat. She was kicking the back of the driver's seat still strapped into her child seat. Her little brother Charlie, Isherwood noticed with a smirk, seemed to be sound asleep, the earlier trumpeting of gunfire notwithstanding.

21

"Sort of, Lu-lu. We're gonna be living at church from now on. We hope." As he spoke to her, he was pushing the brass rounds into the magazine. He thought to himself how his hands were able to do this much faster now than a week ago. Callouses were thickening up his thumbs, too, where he pushed the rounds into place. The pistol was desperately in need of a good oiling. Isherwood had a little burst of excitement as he thought about how the time was coming when he would need to raid a gun store or a hidden cache in one of the nearby homes to start stockpiling weapons and ammunition.

"Living at church?" She repeated. "Church" sounded like "search" in her little voice.

"Yep, it's like God's castle. To protect us from the cut-men."

"Cut-men." Emma nodded, approvingly. "Daddy bang-bang in their face."

"Uh, right." Isherwood said with hesitation. He was always underestimating what she was able to see and absorb. He tried not to think about what all the gore and guts were doing to her little psyche. He was glad that Charlie was able to sleep through it all. Maybe.

Isherwood slid the first magazine back into place. The second one he slid down his back pocket, the same pocket that he used to keep his wallet in. Not much use for wallets anymore.

As he was about the close the driver's side door, Sara came behind him with his Aunt Lizzy along the far side of the car to grab the kids from their child seats. The ladies had apparently finished dispatching the initial wave of zombies from inside the fence. Charlie grumbled as he was dislodged from his seat and then settled back down to sleep in his aunt's arms.

"All right, Emma Claire. Stay looking at mommy. We're gonna go hang out for a minute in Monsignor's back yard, okay?"

"Okay, ma-mommy," the little girl answered and then promptly plugged up her mouth with her thumb.

*****

22

"Ya-know, I think this place'll do just fine." Uncle Jerry was nodding as they walked the perimeter of the church grounds. Isherwood had been rattling the iron bars to begin scattering the mass of zombies that had formed at the church's northeast gate. They were walking counter-clockwise around the church grounds toward the west and back south again, towards the river. The northwestern section of the church grounds was mostly open land, interspersed with tall pine trees. There was another gate here for access to a long steel recyclables container.

"That container might prove useful," Isherwood thought out loud. "Not quite as tall as a container ship container, but it could be used as sort of a panic room in a pinch if things got hairy."

"Would be better if we could move it," Uncle Jerry said. Jerry was pushing into his seventies, but was still incredibly strong. Though his hearing and sight were beginning to fail – Isherwood had been truly lucky only to be nicked by Jerry's shotgun blast – his body was still strong. His skin was long-darkened, either by exposure to the sun and hard work or by the Cajun in his blood. He had worked for the last several decades, as sort of a semi-retirement, in the St. Maryville electric company. Tad – Sara's aunt and Jerry's wife – looked much the same as Jerry in skin tone, but was at least ten years younger. In contrast to Isherwood's Aunt Lizzy and grandmother, Sara's aunt and uncle were going to be much handier to have around, as both were used to living off the land. The apocalypse and the subsequent failure of the electric grid and other modern conveniences really hadn't affected Tad and Jerry's life much, except for the absence of visits from their children and grandchildren, none of whom lived very close by.

They were moving south now, along the west side of the church grounds. There were no gates on this side of the fence. The adjacent property was the Poydras Building and surrounding buildings, which were owned by the city. The Poydras Building used to be Central High School. It was several stories tall and strong, like a fortress, in its own right. It had no fence, though.

"Those warehouses behind Poydras are full of city vehicles, right, Uncle Jerry?"

"What's that?" Jerry said, leaning his ear closer to Isherwood's mouth.

"City vehicles?" Isherwood asked again, pointing to the buildings behind the Poydras building.

"Oh yeah, and a whole maintenance bay full of belts, engine oil, spare tires, and everything we could need to keep a fleet going. That's gonna be a treasure there, boy."

"Nice," Isherwood smiled. They had walked along thousands of feet of fence line and had yet to find a single damaged section. There were several places with diagonal bracing, but Isherwood hardly thought it was necessary. The fence posts themselves were thick as tree trunks in most places, like the Old State Capitol in Baton Rouge.

"Good looking fence, eh?" Isherwood asked Jerry as they came to the southwest corner of the church property where the fence ended about ten feet from the edge of Main Street. They had passed under the shade of an ancient oak tree that stood on the church grounds between the Poydras Building and the church office and Adoration Chapel.

Jerry slapped his thick hand like a bear claw against the post that marked the southwest corner. Jerry's hand made a thudding sound against the solid iron. "Better by a mile than the chain-link at the Kingdom Hall," he answered. The square post was taller than either of the two men, over seven feet, and served also as a pedestal for a sculpture of a winged lion.

As they turned to the east, all of Main Street and downtown St. Maryville unfolded before them.

"Crap." Isherwood said, and was echoed by Uncle Jerry's more explicit phrasing. "Good thing we took the side streets." Isherwood continued. The mobs weren't thick directly in front of the church where a statue of Jesus – "Touchdown Jesus," most called it – looked across the road to the entrance of St. Mary's. Behind the statue of Jesus the land fell away steeply to a boat launch, the main entrance to False River. No doubt the steepness of the incline helped thin the crowd of staggering, sometimes off balance, zombies. Much further on, however, the crowds grew thick, so thick they blocked the rest of the view of Main Street.

"Guess we won't be grocery shopping at Langlois'." Isherwood remarked. Six blocks further east was the grocery store at the front of Delware Avenue, the other end of which they had just come from. "I'd only snuck in the grocery at night and from the back – I never realized *this* is what Main Street looked like."

"It might be getting worse, too – those things seem to attract one another." Jerry added. "We ought to keep a lower profile even behind this fence."

"Let's just check the two gates in front of the church office, and we can fade to black after that. They seem to be the only weak parts of the whole fence line."

"There's one more gate after these, ain't there?" Jerry asked.

"Yeah, the east side has one gate. We might be able to get to it without getting noticed if we go around the back of the church. We'll be skipping the southeast corner, but if we don't see any of those things staggering across the lawn, it'll be a good bet that part of the fence line is solid as the rest. Ah, crap – there's one more set of gates we'd be skipping over. The *front* gates, right in front of the main doors of the church."

"All right. We'll be fine if we stick together. I haven't heard a peep from the women-folk, so they've probably found their way inside the fence of the rectory. That line of trees and landscaping should get us close enough to the front gates without them things being none the wiser."

*****

"Crap." Isherwood said again, after they had crawled and crunched their way through the inside of some giant formosa azalea bushes. They had their backs against a three-sided low brick wall that served as a planting bed for flowers and a small crape myrtle tree. "Are you seeing what I'm seeing?"

Isherwood pointed to a place midway up the right front gate, and was again echoed by Uncle Jerry's more explicit phrasing. "Maybe Tattoo wigged out and made a break for it." The gate was only slightly ajar. Oddly, it was open towards Main Street, so it was unlikely that many zombies, if any at all, had wandered inward. "The padlock's just hanging there."

"Is the padlock hanging open?" Jerry asked, unable to see for himself.

"Yes. Just dangling there." Isherwood answered.

"That's luck."

"We're less than fifteen feet away. I could sprint over there, shut the gate, and lock it, before any of those things noticed, much less got to me. Heck, it's a decent angle. I might be able to get away without notice altogether."

"Do it, kid." Jerry agreed. "Do it before our luck runs out. I'll cover you." Isherwood winced at the idea of the shotgun being aimed near him again. "But, Ish – don't sprint. Just mosey over there real easy like, and they might just think you're a dead-head, too."

At the count of three, Isherwood slowly rose up from behind cover. As he stood there and quietly began moving toward the gate, he noticed that none of them were noticing him. This had worked for him during his night time raids, but he had never really tried it in the daylight. Within moments, he was standing at the gate and pulling it towards him. It was heavy. Too heavy. The creaking might as well have been a blast from a fog horn – or a dinner bell. Half of Main Street swung their heads his way.

"Come on, kid!" Uncle Jerry said, cussing. Isherwood's hands began shaking violently as he fumbled with the padlock. A hand fell atop his own, and he was looking eye to eye at a rotting teenage girl. Only her stringy hair could pass between the iron bars, but she was tugging on his hand. He couldn't forcefully push her away, so Isherwood dragged her arm inside the posts and snapped in sideways, rendering it unusable. He then pushed it back out of the gate. It was horrible, Isherwood thought, as he watched the girl's eyes through their little exchange, how the pain didn't even register on their faces.

Isherwood swung the creaking gate so that its iron ring overlapped the matching ring of the post. He slipped the padlock through the union and closed it with a click. Though the padlock was joining to other sturdy pieces of metal, he thought to himself that the spot will likely need to be reinforced soon. With the few moments he had left before more of those things stumbled over, he pulled out a few long strips of black plastic from his pockets, which he had brought for just this purpose. Zip ties. They could seal up a chain link fence against zombies no problem, but they weren't yet tested on iron posts. He zipped them tight at three places along the length of the post. *That'll hafta do for now*, he thought to himself as Uncle Jerry's thick arm began dragging him backward.

CHAPTER FOUR:
THE RECTORY

"Your husband just made sure that fence is gonna get field tested in a hurry." Uncle Jerry added, somewhat loudly, to the hushed discussion that was ongoing in the backyard of the rectory.

"So y'all haven't seen any sign of anything moving inside the rectory?" Isherwood asked. "Have you even tried knocking?"

"No and *no* – you made me promise you I wouldn't knock until you got back. Remember?" Sara scolded.

"Oh, yeah." The wave of crimson again washed over Isherwood's face. "Well, any reason I shouldn't get on with it?" He looked from face to face. Sara was shaking her head, as Emma squirmed in her arms. Emma's thigh had been reddened with spanks, after she had started screaming for Sara to let her down. Isherwood's aunt and grandmother were wavering on their feet with unfocused eyes, probably in some minor state of shock. Aunt Lizzy was still holding Charlie and he was *still* sleeping.

Aunt Tad was standing with the shotgun slung over one arm and holding Uncle Jerry's arm with the other. "Nah, honey. Let's get on with it. Bet they've got nice beds in there, and I wouldn't mind putting my head down. Might even get a good night's sleep tonight behind that nice fence."

"Agreed." Isherwood nodded. He turned to the rectory's back door that opened into the backyard from the kitchen. He knocked on it a few times, but there was no answer or sound from the house. He leaned over a metal railing to peak inside the kitchen window. "I'm not seeing anything. There are more doors – one on every side of the house. Let's not split up, though."

"Well," Sara whispered. "The good news is – if we haven't heard anything yet, it's probably not a zombie inside. It's either empty or Monsignor is sleeping or Monsignor is more deaf than we realized."

"*Or*," Isherwood said. "He's more deaf than we realize because he just fired a rifle to save my butt." Uncle Jerry grumbled in agreement. "Yeah, let's see if we can pry this door open. Sara, why don't you throw some pebbles at the upstairs window while I do this. Hate to ruin a perfectly good door and lock these days."

The pebbles having done no good, Isherwood was able to pry open the door a few minutes later. In a moment, they were all in the kitchen of the rectory. Isherwood put the door back together as best he could and latched it. "Everybody just stay here in the kitchen a second, okay?" Isherwood went into the large dining room adjacent to the kitchen and grabbed a chair. He left Monsignor's chair untouched at the head of the table.

"Looks like somebody's been using this kitchen," Gran said. "A living person, I mean."

"I think this is the first time I've been in the rectory." Aunt Lizzy said.

"I know it's my first time." Aunt Tad said with a note of derision. She and Uncle Jerry had both grown up Catholic, but had since bounced through various non-denominational and Pentecostal congregations.

"There. That should hold for now." Isherwood said as he wedged the dining room chair under the doorknob of the kitchen door. "The rest of the doors – except for maybe the screen door on the side porch – are old and heavy and should withstand anything."

"Good, because Charlie's starting to stir." Aunt Lizzy said.

"Yeah, and Emma's about to go mad. She wants to get down and run around."

"Almost." Isherwood said. "Let me sweep the house first."

"And, Isherwood. I don't understand," Gran said. "Why are you so worried about the doors? I thought you said the fence would hold."

"It's a fine fence." Uncle Jerry agreed.

"It will hold, Gran." Isherwood nodded. "But, we're gonna need several layers of fortification, you know what I mean? The fence is the first layer, though I have plans for pushing beyond the fence. The buildings are the second layer, and the church building, itself, is the last layer, the castle keep, sorta."

"Pushing beyond the fence?" Sara asked.

"Yeah, we've talked about it." Isherwood said with a hint of annoyance. "But let me sweep the house. I've probably waited too long already."

"The house is clear," a new voice said. "And welcome!"

Everybody spun toward the entrance to the kitchen, where a tall old priest was leaning against the door frame and smiling. "Monsignor!" Sara exclaimed, and Emma finally burst from her grasp, running to grab at Monsignor's knees.

"Oh, hello, Emma." Monsignor stooped down to hold the little girl's hands as she jumped on his broad, clunky shoes. "And did you bring little Andrew with you?"

"*Charlie*, Monsignor," Aunt Lizzy said, still holding the boy. Charlie had started waving and clapping his arms around madly ever since Monsignor's appearance. She lowered the boy down and he crawled over, his little hands and knees slapping loudly on the hardwood floor, to Monsignor and his sister.

"Charlie! That's right. I always do that. And how is little Charlie?" The little boy answered by slapping the priest's worn black shoes. "So glad to see all of you still alive."

30

"So that *was* you with the rifle?" Isherwood asked. He sounded a bit like a little boy, as he said it.

"I suppose it could've been," Monsignor answered with his characteristic half smile. "So let's sit down," he said, ushering his guests into the dining room. "I want to hear about your plans, Isherwood, to make this place into a castle, as well as your plans beyond this place. A little bird has been telling me that you would soon be stopping by. And I need to meet these two."

"This is my Aunt Tad and Uncle Jerry," Sara answered. "That's my dad's sister."

"We're all neighbors," Gran explained.

"I see," Monsignor nodded. "Mrs. Lorio and Ms. Lorio," he said, bending to acknowledge Isherwood's Gran and Aunt Lizzy. "It wasn't long ago that we buried your husband, as I remember. It's good he was spared from all this madness. Would that we all could have been."

"Where's Tattoo?" Sara said suddenly. She had sat down with the rest of them at the table. There was a chair missing anyway. She was following the two kids around, slowly child-proofing the first floor of the rectory, which was filled with valuable breakables. "I thought he'd be with you."

"Oh, he comes and goes. I'm sure he'll be fine."

"I think he ran out through the front gate," Isherwood said. "He could've ruined everything. Those things could've packed in here, but we were lucky. If he wants back in, Tatoo'll hafta find another way. I sealed that gate up tight."

Monsignor nodded at the head of the table. His eyes were hidden beneath his deep brow, which bore a broad divot of a scar. "They, those things, I mean. They don't really like this place, thankfully. I think we can all guess why." Everybody around the table exchanged meaningful glances. "And don't worry about Tattoo. He'll find a way in if he wants. He always does. But tell me about your plans for this place, Isherwood."

"Yeah, Isherwood," Sara added. "I thought I knew your plan, but I think you must be thinking more than you're saying. You know how you tend to do that. Optimizing, always optimizing."

Lizzy laughed to herself. "I remember the days when he said more than he thought."

Isherwood blushed, but was eager to share his plans. He raised his eyes to the large framed map above the mantle of the dining room's fireplace. He shook his head in surprise. "Huh," he said smiling. "That's exactly what I was just hoping to find. I was just going to ask you for a map, Monsignor, and there one is. Excellent."

"Wow," Sara smiled. "It's like the old place wants us to help fight back."

"Awesome," Isherwood smiled back at his wife. "Well, look guys. I think we can make a stand here at the church. But what's more, I think this place could be just the sort of seed that could start civilization over again. Sort of like how humanity receded back to within the monasteries after the bubonic plague in the middle ages. You see? The branch that will shoot up from the stump of Jesse? Look here." He traced the shape of False River on the map. "See how the lake – there's False river there – makes a wide crescent at the front of the church and the Mississippi River sorta makes a wide crescent at the back of the church? St. Maryville is sort of like an island, see? The river used to run around us on either side, but now False River is cut off from the river, there and there."

"Now," Isherwood continued. "We've got to think about how the zombies will begin to spread out over time. That means that millions and millions of those things will start spreading out from Baton Rouge and New Orleans, they'll be coming up I-10 right for us, though it'll take time for it to happen. In the meantime, though, we can easily isolate ourselves. We can make an island out of St. Maryville, do you see it? There's only three ways into St. Maryville: on either side of False River, where it doesn't quite reach the Mississippi anymore, and the Audubon Bridge. We could easily block these three places, enough, at least, to help direct the zombie hordes westward as they migrate."

"The kingdom of St. Maryville," Monsignor smiled, leaning backward in his chair. "A fine plan, Isherwood." The rest murmured their agreement.

Isherwood was trying poorly to conceal his excitement. "Layers of fences within fences. Islands within islands. Get it? There's more, too. Sara gave me this idea. We still need to get rid of all the zombies inside the … the, uh … *kingdom* of St. Maryville." Isherwood went on to explain how they would need to trap what cattle and other animals they could find within rings of punji sticks to draw in and stick the zombies, while also protecting the livestock.

"No offense, but it looks like I'm the only able-bodied one among us."

"Hey!" Sara protested.

"Oh yeah. If some of you can help us with the kids, that would free up Sara to help me. Besides, I think that pretty much everybody could help with the punji sticks."

"Don't you think we should start with the punji sticks right here around the fence, so the zombies can't start pushing in and weakening it?" Sara asked.

"Couldn't we just spear their heads from inside the fences?" Aunt Tad asked.

"I thought about that," Isherwood said. "If we did that, their carcasses would start mounding up against the fences, and they could start climbing in. It's like what the Romans did at Mosada."

"What?" Sara asked.

"Nevermind." Isherwood shook his head. "Forget Mosada. But we need to use punji sticks to help us keep weight off the fences and stop them from encircling and trapping us. Y'all understand?"

"All those zombie movies you watched growing up are finally coming in handy," Lizzy started laughing.

"I still don't get why you loved those movies," Gran said rubbing her temple.

"Even now?" Isherwood asked.

"*Especially* now!" Gran laughed, and they all joined in laughing.

Monsignor pushed his chair back from the table and lifted himself up with some effort. "I better go put on a kettle of water. The stove is still working. It's gas. I think we're going to need some coffee to finish going over Mr. Smith's plans. They appear *quite* extensive."

"Water?" Isherwood asked. "I meant to ask before. There's got to be an old well somewhere on the property, right?"

"Why don't you start making a to-do list, honey?" Sara whispered in her husband's ear. "Everybody's pretty tired. You know, all this mess with zombies and the end of the world actually tires *some* people out."

CHAPTER FIVE: MORNING

It wasn't much longer before Isherwood's seemingly unending list of ideas plus the excitement and fear of the day led to drooping eyelids around the table. Even Emma and Charlie were soon curling up on the rug beneath the dining room table, snoring softly at their mother's feet.

The rectory had been home to only one or two priests at a time for nearly fifty years, so there was plenty of extra space for the newcomers, if not extra beds. Besides the kitchen and dining room, the first floor included a large study and two parlors. The larger parlor held a grand piano. Monsignor's mother had been a music teacher, and the priest was still a talented pianist despite his arthritic hands. There were also broad couches and rugs. The parlor became Uncle Jerry's and Aunt Tad's room.

Lizzy and Gran moved into the smaller parlor. Both Gran and her daughter were on the shorter side, so the two couches were large enough. Gran was also a very light sleeper. Even more so now that the dead had starting walking. She agreed to be something of a watch dog for the house. She preferred to be near the kitchen, anyway, and Lizzy preferred to be near her mother.

Everyone agreed it was best for the children to stay upstairs, where their crying would be more muffled, so the Smith family moved into the spare bedroom. Monsignor stayed in his own bedroom.

Isherwood didn't know how many more people could be housed on the church property, but it could be dozens. Despite the rectory and the church building, itself, there was the parish hall, the St. Joseph's Center, and the church office. He knew from childhood church lock-ins that the parish hall could house about a hundred rampaging children. With cots laid out and sheets strung up for walls, it could house probably ten to fifteen families. Both the parish hall and church office had their own kitchens, as well. The church office had about a dozen separate rooms and offices, each of which could be used for long-term housing. The church, itself, could house hundreds of people in the pews for a short time.

If there were even that many people left in town, that was.

*****

Isherwood and Gran were waiting for the rest, drinking coffee, when morning came. They were sitting at the counter in the kitchen, instead of the dining room table, so as not to wake Aunt Lizzy in the side parlor. Their efforts had apparently succeeded, as Lizzy was still snoring loudly.

"You and me, drinking coffee," Isherwood smiled, as Gran slurped her coffee. "It's always been this way, hasn't it?"

"Even as a little boy, you'd wake up before dawn," Gran nodded. "We'd drink coffee. You, coffee milk, of course. You'd say I sounded like Darth Vader drinking my coffee."

"It's nice that coffee is vacuum-sealed," Isherwood thought aloud. "It could be a generation before we run out of it."

"It's nice to feel safe again. Somewhat safe, anyway."

Safety is just an illusion. Isherwood thought to himself. He would not say this to his Gran, whose heart, he knew, had grown weak. *But every little bit of illusion will keep her alive longer.*

"I hope I'll be able to find us more people," Isherwood said. "Maybe a couple more men."

"There's safety in numbers. It's always been that way. Especially now that that is *their* greatest strength."

"The zombies?" he asked.

"I don't like that word. The 'creatures,' I call them."

"Yeah, numbers and will power, if you can call it that," Isherwood took a turn slurping his coffee.

"A generation, huh?" Gran asked. "You're thinking pretty far ahead, aren't you?"

"Of course. The present is survival, which is impossible without the future, which is hope. Without that, they win. Somehow our will has to be stronger than theirs."

"Is that why you brought us *here*, then? It wasn't just for the fence, was it?" Gran asked. "Isherwood," she said, suddenly changing her tone. "It may not always be enough to have a flurry of ideas. Even if they're really good ideas. For people to follow you, I mean. Hard choices will eventually come. You won't be able to save everybody. *You* can't save everybody. I know you've been having dreams, though, haven't you? There's more at work here than just you. But now we have Monsignor, and that is good. Soon more like him will come, too."

Isherwood didn't look at his grandmother. He felt frozen, staring down into his coffee. He could smell the hard edge of coffee on her breath. She was speaking very close to him now. It irritated him, somehow. He felt like he was a little boy again and the nagging would get in his way, as it used to.

"What I'm trying to say is this. There will come a time when you'll run out of ideas. It might still be a ways off, but it *will* happen. Just know that it's okay. You're part of something that may work equally well without your ideas. Because you are more than your work. *A lot* more."

Isherwood still didn't answer, lowering his head to his coffee. Gran knew that a certain part of him had withdrawn from her for now and would be wrestling with what she had said.

"Gran?" He finally asked as a surge of caffeine reinflated his spirits. "You're good at canning and preserving, right, Gran?"

"Ah, I see you've got a job for me."

"We'll start with getting all the canned goods that we can here," Isherwood said. He was off again on his mission. "The parish hall will be good for that. We'll have to hide some, too, in case we get raided. Hidden caches in town, maybe. But if the electricity held out long enough, there may still be some meat and other frozen goods that haven't spoiled. I'll definitely need your help canning all that."

"I'll help with that, too, Ishy. Your Gran and I will be canning queens," Aunt Tad said, walking barefoot into the kitchen to join them. "I have to thank you, Ish, for one of the best night's sleep I've had in a long time, since all this happened. There's something about this place. I never would've thought that I'd leave my house on Delaware Avenue, let alone feel safer somewhere else."

"I thought the exact thing, Tad," Gran agreed, pouring and handing her old neighbor a cup of coffee. "It's nice to see what good can come from tragedy. I can't remember the last time we shared a cup of coffee and just look at us."

"Amen, Jesus. That's right, dear." Tad squeezed the old woman tightly. "So, Ishy, what are your plans for the day? I now you've got a few ... *dozen*." She and Gran erupted in laughter. Gran squeezed and shook Tad's knee with her small hand.

"Shh," Isherwood scolded, though the women barely heard him over the sound of their rapturous laughter. "You'll wake *the dead*."

*****

True to form, Isherwood did have a plan. Within the hour, he had awakened Uncle Jerry and convinced him to relocate his truck to the front lawn of the rectory.

"Did they hear you move your truck over to the gate by the Poydras building?" Isherwood asked as Uncle Jerry returned to the rectory through the side porch. Everybody was again seated at the dining room table.

"Of course they did," Jerry growled. "Thing's diesel. Might as well ring the church bells. Whole damn town is starting to converge at our front door step."

"Good!" Isherwood nodded, as the color drained from the faces of everybody else at the table. "That's perfect. Here's what we're gonna do. Everyone stays here except for me and Jerry. Sara and Aunt Tad, you're in charge of protecting this place when we leave. Monsignor, get your rifle. Gran and Aunt Lizzy will stay here in the rectory and keep the kids quiet."

"But if you were just gonna sneak off to Wal-Mart for supplies, why get the attention of the whole Main Street horde?" Sara demanded, angrily.

"You know me, Sara. I'm trying to kill as many stones as possible with one bird. I mean, as many birds as possible, well, zombies, actually …"

"We got it." Sara cut him short.

"Look," Isherwood began again. "Remember how I wanted to cut off the Audubon Bridge? To start making this place an island? Well, this may be super risky, since we haven't already scouted out the situation on the bridge. But we're gonna lead that horde across the bridge and a few miles beyond, retreat back the way we came, and then block the bridge behind us."

"That's not just risky. That's *insane*," Sara screamed.

"It *would* clean out the town," Monsignor nodded approvingly.

"Wait, what?" Sara said. "You're not agreeing with this are you? How're they supposed to come back across the bridge once the road is clogged with a mile of zombies? What if the bridge is blocked somewhere along the way? What if they run out of gas?"

"We've got a couple extra gas cans all filled up in the bed," Uncle Jerry added.

"And I've already thought through the backtracking part, too, Sara. There's a divider in the roadway, tall enough, I think, to keep all the zombies in one lane while we drive up the other side."

"But, Isherwood," Gran said. "What will you use to block the bridge? Cars? Where will you get enough?"

"Yeah, that's a tricky spot," Isherwood nodded. "I did watch a bunch of videos on YouTube before the electricity ran out. Several on hot-wiring cars. I think I can do it."

"Hot-wiring?" Uncle Jerry asked. "That old truck of mine's been hot-wired for years. One of our kids lost the keys during the Clinton administration, and old Tad over there was too cheap to buy new ones. Hot-wiring's easy. I got you there."

"Whoa, really?" Isherwood said, relieved. "That's awesome. Thank *God*. Though I did have a back-up idea of raiding the car dealership. They keep all their keys in a wall box in the general manager's office. Of course, I wouldn't be able to do that without drawing attention until the horde cleared out, so that would mean Uncle Jerry driving alone most of the way."

"It's probably best that you only venture out in pairs," Monsignor insisted.

"We really need radios," Isherwood said, sighing. Cell phone service had been one of the first parts of civilization to come tumbling down.

"Once you clear out all those zombies," Lizzy chimed in. "We'll be able to grab whatever we want from wherever we want. We'll have a little shopping spree."

"Okay, fine," Sara said. "But, Smith, you better talk all this over with me next time, *step by step*, before you even think about starting the truck. You understand me?"

Isherwood moved his chair closer to his wife's. He put his arm around her. Though she resisted at first, she eventually let him embrace her. "I'm coming back, okay? And when I do, this place will be a lot safer, for *all* of us."

*****

"Okay, guys, so we only got one chance at this." Isherwood was standing with Sara, Tad, and Jerry between the rectory and the church building, where a screen of trees concealed them in front of the St. Joseph's Building. Gran and Lizzy were still in the rectory with the kids, and they could just see Monsignor's rifle sticking out the screened window of his upstairs bedroom. "Uncle Jerry's letting the truck run in front of the rectory," Isherwood continued. "That should get them massing up. It's looking and sounding great. The fence, I mean. That leaves the westernmost gate down there relatively zombie-free. We should be able to drive through the grass and parking lots and through the gate before they can get there."

"So, Tad and Sara, y'all will slip behind the buildings, keeping a low profile, and approach the gate from behind the Adoration Chapel, while we grab their attention, got it?"

"You sure you don't want to take the second CRV?" Sara asked. Her voice was shaking with fear and adrenaline at seeing so many of those things in one place.

Isherwood shook his head. "If all goes right, I'm hoping we'll be returning with an extra vehicle, *especially* now that I know Uncle Jerry can hotwire. We might even pass by the dealership on the way back." The young man's eyes glinted at the prospect, and Sara noticed it. She knew her husband had been itching for the kind of shopping sprees that only the apocalypse could offer. And even though they completely worthless now and madness to risk a life for, Sara also knew that Isherwood secretly had his eye out for a baseball card stash.

Sara grabbed his arm, taking him aside. She walked him over to the side door of the rectory, where they would still be screened by the trees and palms. "Look, Isherwood," she said. She was having trouble controlling her voice, while trying to hold back tears. "I just need to make sure that you're not taking needless risks and leaving us here without you. I know that look in your eye."

Isherwood reacted with irritation. He was feeling the tension of time, but more than that he was exhilarated by the challenge. The excitement he was feeling seemed to evaporate at Sara's words. "I gotta get going," he said through gritted teeth. But Sara held him back.

"Isherwood," she said. "This isn't some zombie fantasy, okay? This is real, and your family really needs you."

"I *know*, alright?" Isherwood said, sounding exhausted. "*That's* why I'm doing this. We've gotta clear out the town or nobody will be safe here for long. Eventually, they'll just overwhelm that fence."

Just before Sara could respond, a little voice came from a crack in the side door of the rectory. "Ma-daddy? ky-it, ma-daddy. *Shhh*."

"Em-*ma* Claire," Sara yelled quietly. "Get *back* in that house. *Gran! Aunt Lizzy!* Come grab Emmy."

"We got it, Ishy," Tad said, motioning with a shotgun. "Let's get going before they put much more strain on that fence."

"Alright," Sara said, after getting her daughter back under supervision and making sure the doors were locked. Her face was flushed and she disciplined a loose strand of hair back behind her ear. "Alright, let's do this. You're coming back through the northwest gate, right?"

"Right," Isherwood said, somewhat chastened. "The one by the recyclables container. Okay, let's go." Isherwood kissed his wife and squeezed her hard. Both couples exchanged 'I love you's.' Isherwood then stepped out from behind cover and started making straight for the fence and the waiting truck. Jerry followed behind him. He was waving his arms to get the zombies' attention. The moaning was starting to grow louder. There was little need for that and no need to yell and make sounds, as the loud diesel-engined truck had been left running.

"Sure hope this works, kid." Jerry said, as they climbed into the cab of the old F-250, and slammed their doors behind them. They waited there for a few seconds as Sara and Tad made their way to the far gate.

"So do I," Isherwood agreed with a dry mouth. "No need to go slowly once the ladies are in position, faster the better for their sake. They're dim-witted and slow, but the zombies will catch up soon enough."

Sara and Tad crept out from behind the far side of the Adoration Chapel. Aunt Tad kept a few yards of distance from the gate, as Sara ran for the padlock.

"Here we go!" Uncle Jerry announced, and Isherwood couldn't help but notice the growl of excitement in his voice. For his part, Isherwood choked down the fear in his belly and grabbed the handle above the door.

They bumped up and down over several curbs to drive across the front of the rectory and chapel. Just as they arrived in the last parking lot to make the turn out the gate, Sara had the gate sliding open. She opened it just enough for the truck to pass. She and Isherwood exchanged a quick glance as they passed each other. *God, she's beautiful,* he thought to himself, before getting distracted. The distraction was not a zombie, but a smallish man darting back through the gate.

"Was that Tattoo?" Isherwood called out.

"What's that?" Jerry asked. With his poor hearing, he was barely able to distinguish between the truck and Isherwood.

"Nothing, nothing," he said, looking backward, as the little man disappeared into the church grounds. Sara and Tad motioned to him not to worry, then gave him "okay" signs as the gate slid back into place before the first zombie was even ten yards away.

The truck stood idling along Main Street in front of the Poydras Building, waiting for the horde to catch up. Isherwood watched as Sara and Tad disappeared back behind cover. He thought he might have caught a glimpse of them just as they reached the rectory.

He then turned his attention fully on the three hundred or so glazed and scratched eyes staring at him from the road. Now that they had seen live flesh, the moaning was growing deafening. Isherwood thought how Civil War historians had struggled to describe the sound of the Rebel battle yell. Those that heard it, they said, never forgot it. He thought the moans of the undead must be like this. It wasn't that it sounded inhuman; it still sounded *very* human. It was a grotesque perversion of a human voice, amplified by a thousand rotting throats.

Isherwood shook his head. "Well," he yelled above the moans and the engine noise, forcing his thoughts back to the job at hand. "This will be slow-going, but hopefully that means simple."

"What route're we takin'?" Jerry asked.

"Major Parkway. We might even be able to raid the Shell station before we turn north."

"Keep it simple kid. One stone, four hundred birds is good enough for one morning."

Sara's words rang in his head just then: *optimizing, always optimizing.* "Alright, Uncle Jerry. Okay."

Not long thereafter, Jerry budged the truck forward. Isherwood settled into his plan, checking and rechecking his two pistol magazines before climbing out the back window into the bed of the truck. He had brought along five 50-round boxes of 9mm ammo. He kept three within arm's reach through the rear window along the back seat of the truck, and the other two he kept in the bed with him. He also had a battery-powered loudspeaker that he had borrowed from the youth group office at the church.

There was no need to use pillows to suppress the sound of his pistol this morning. Though he wished he had one of Sara's nice-smelling pillows to breathe through. The stench was overwhelming. When the wind would suddenly shift upstream of the horde, Isherwood felt like he could smell every one of them. The rotting meat quivered as they staggered forward. Sometimes, he even saw little clumps of maggots drop to the ground, a packet of them dislodged from inside a gaping wound. He kept firing to keep the smell of gunpowder in the air, not just to keep their attention.

For the most part, he saved his bullets for the zombies that got too close to the back tailgate and sides of the truck. He was getting to know his pistol really well with all the extra practice. He was about 50/50 for headshots at forty yards, but was lethal within twenty-five, even from the bed of the moving truck.

It was unnerving, while they were going so slow, watching the hundreds of zombies staggering after them. The speedometer said they were going just under ten miles per hour. When Isherwood thought he could almost recognize the individual faces, most of whom he'd grown up knowing, they were getting too close. Every couple hundred yards or so, Isherwood would tap the window for Jerry to give the truck a little extra speed.

He would go mad if he had to stare back at them, eye-to-eye, from the back of this truck for much longer. The lake was trailing along the left side of the road. It appeared like flashes of green between adjacent houses. He would turn and stare out across it. It was so calm, he half-expected to see jet-skis roaring across it.

The first time Isherwood turned on the loudspeaker it sounded preternaturally loud, like the roar of some sea beast rising from the lake. The zombies actually stopped in their tracks when they first heard the ping of Isherwood switching it on. The moaning stopped for an instant, like a sudden gap in the water coming out of a faucet. But they lurched ahead in redoubled madness after the momentary shock had worn off.

"Anybody in St. Maryville," Isherwood's voice squeaked out. He cleared his throat and started again, "Survivors, this is Isherwood Smith. We're drawing the zombies across the bridge. Stay perfectly still until the horde passes you by. When the coast is clear, join us at St. Mary's Church, our temporary shelter. Bring your supplies." He repeated the same message every couple of minutes, though the sound seemed to drown in the sea of moans.

CHAPTER SIX:
THE SNAKE

Looking around at all the grand, older homes along Main Street, Isherwood was sad to see many with open doors and broken windows. He was sadder still to see zombies stumbling out of most of these homes to follow them. Main Street seemed to be the hardest hit. Hopefully, he thought, the sound of his megaphone would carry down the side streets, as well, and would be heard by *somebody*.

After what seemed like an eternity, but had only been about fifteen minutes, the old red truck finally turned away from the lake and north onto Major Parkway. A few hundred yards west of this intersection lay the intersection of Main Street and Hospital Road, the other stoplight on Main Street. Most of the larger businesses in town lay along Hospital Road, including the Winn-Dixie, the Wal-Mart, and all the fast food restaurants. Isherwood also expected a second and larger horde of zombies was occupying this road, some of which they might be able to draw off today across the bridge. Or else, it might be waiting for them, having migrated eastward, if they came the same way along Major Parkway – Isherwood had specifically designed his plan to avoid this, and, incidentally, to pass by both of the car dealerships in town.

"Alright, let's kick this hornet's nest!" Isherwood called to Uncle Jerry to accelerate the truck up Major Parkway to where it intersected with a side street that connected to the back of Wal-Mart. Between the intersection and Wal-Mart on either side of the road, there were fields of sugar cane still growing in the fields. The land along the western side of Major Parkway, along the backs of the Wal-Mart and strip malls, was still undeveloped farmland, almost a hundred acres all together.

At the intersection, which also didn't require a stoplight, there was a three-story brick technological services building, called the Washburn Building, and a nursing home that was still under construction when the Atlantic and Pacific seaboards got hit with the first waves of zombies. On the east side of Major Parkway was Major subdivision, which Isherwood actually hoped was empty because his plan might inadvertently overrun the subdivision with zombies.

He had friends that lived in this subdivision, some of his best friends. He had tried to contact them early on, but couldn't reach them. Last he heard, they had bugged out early, abandoning town. Wherever they ended up, he hoped they would somehow meet up again, maybe even return home to St. Maryville.

When they reached the intersection, they had put perhaps three hundred yards of distance between themselves and the Main Street horde. He made another announcement on his megaphone, specifically directed to Major subdivision. "Get in your vehicles immediately and come with us, leaving everything behind, or else stay very quiet as the horde passes you by." Afterwards, Isherwood asked Jerry to lay on the horn.

Isherwood stood up in the bed of the truck as it idled. There were about twenty or so zombies that were close enough to be threats. Isherwood took careful aim, trying to ease his nerves which were beginning to prickle all up and down his back like a bad rash. He could feel something approaching from the west. A new wave of moans soon rolled over them.

"Here they come!" Isherwood said to Jerry, though he knew the old man couldn't hear him over the din of the horn and moans. As they both watched, a grey haze formed around Wal-Mart and at the end of the road leading to it. It was like a low-creeping fog moving along the horizon. It seemed to be still, but when they blinked they could tell it was moving. The color drained from their faces at the sheer size of the horde coming up from Wal-Mart and Hospital Road. Even Jerry's dark-tinted Cajun skin seemed ghost-like.

Isherwood spun around as a new sound erupted nearby. *What had he missed?* A string of thoughts pulsed through his mind. It was another car horn. *Another truck? Two trucks? Zombies don't drive trucks*, he thought to himself stupidly.

"Hey, buddy," a voice announced nonchalantly from the first truck, actually a brown Chevy Tahoe. It was one of Isherwood's old friends from his days teaching at the local Catholic school. He pulled up his vehicle forward out of Major subdivision. Kids stirred in the back seats. Though his wife sat petrified in the passenger seat, the driver looked as calm as a Sunday driver.

"Patrick *O'Hooligan*," Isherwood cried out, temporarily oblivious to their impending catastrophe. Patrick had an almost supernatural way of putting people at ease. He taught English to middle schoolers, who were themselves each tiny maelstroms of hormones and chaos. Isherwood always admired Patrick's zen-like ability to remain serene at the center of a chaotic classroom. Patrick's name was Patrick, but not O'Hooligan. It was Patrick Fontenot. He was a track coach as well as a teacher.

Isherwood turned to face another blur of movement coming out of the neighborhood. "And look who else decided to show his ugly face."

"Thought you'd take on the apocalypse all by yourself, did you?" The driver of the second truck, a blue Chevy, called out.

"Justin, you idiot." The second driver was Justin Chustz. His wife, Chelsea, waved hesitantly from the passenger seat. Their faces looked emaciated, and they seemed to be hiding terror just under their voices.

"What took you so long?" Justin called back. "We were about to run out of steak and beer."

"You poor, stupid fools," Isherwood called back. "Never been so happy to see anybody ... you heard me just now and got in your trucks?"

"Hey, Ish?" Chelsea interrupted, leaning across the center console. "Sara and the kids? They all made it?" Isherwood assured her that his whole family was intact and waiting at the church. Their wives had been friends far longer than Isherwood and Justin had. Relief washed across Chelsea's face.

"We heard you back when you passed by the Shell station, I think," Patrick called back. "Pretty quiet these days. Sound travels easy. Oh, yeah, and the apocalypse of moans coming this way was hard to miss. You actually didn't give us much of a choice, buddy."

"Sorry about that," Isherwood grimaced. "It made the choice pretty easy, though, right? So, uh, y'all got the gist of the plan? Lead the pukes over the bridge, circle back, block the bridge. Got it?"

"What could go wrong?" Justin asked sarcastically. "Come out to the coast, we'll get together, have a few laughs…"

A clanging sound sparked against the tailgate of Jerry's truck. "What the …?" Isherwood spun around.

"Better take care of that, Smith," Patrick called out. His calm voice held just a hint of an edge.

It was the leading edge of the Main Street horde. Isherwood popped off five or six rounds until his magazine clicked empty, and then switched out magazines. As he did, four or five zombies fell onto their knees or toppled backwards. With the fresh magazine, he finished off the troublemakers and turned back to Jerry. "Alright, punch it," he yelled into the cab.

"Y'all armed?" Isherwood asked as he passed by his friends' vehicles.

Patrick shook his head. Justin, however, heaved an AR-15 out his window. "Don't leave home without it," Justin smiled.

"Alrighty," Isherwood smiled back. "Patrick, you take the middle spot. Justin, you okay with the caboose?"

"No problemo," Justin shouted back. "My kids will take over for you, too." As he said it, a boy and a girl spilled out from the back window of the blue Chevy. Though Justin kept the Armalite rifle for himself, his kids each had .22 rifles. Isherwood saluted in answer, and turned back to face the front of the truck. They were about to pass the

Scott Civic Center, where Isherwood and Sara had had their wedding reception several years ago. From there, they would cross over the hump of railroad tracks. The foot of the bridge was another two, two-and-a-half miles after the railroad tracks. They were approaching a little intersection connecting Major Parkway, Parent Street, which was basically the Main Street of the back half of St. Maryville, and Highway 1. Once they cleared this intersection and St. Maryville's last stoplight, it was just open four-lane highway with wide shoulders and even wider lanes of grass on either side before fences rose to cut off the pasture lands and stretches of timber beyond.

Even if we can't get them over the bridge, Isherwood thought to himself as he stood in the bed of the truck, *they'll be as good as trapped inside all these fences. Maybe. Hopefully. It will definitely confuse them.*

Isherwood took one last lingering look across the farmland that stood along the west side of Major Parkway. Beyond these fields lay the backs of the stores that faced Hospital Road. The largest of these stores stood out along the horizon. It was Wal-Mart. If they got through this, Isherwood promised himself, he would soon be back. This Wal-Mart, he knew, held a good supply of guns and ammunition. He was itching to go shopping.

*****

Isherwood tapped on the cab of Jerry's red truck and raised his hand to slow the trucks behind him. They stopped just past the last stoplight before leaving St. Maryville. The road ahead was completely empty, except for a couple cars abandoned here and there along the side of the road. *Probably,* Isherwood thought, *with a zombie still seat-belted in the backseat, reaching and groping at us as we pass by. Likely, a person that was bitten and never quite made it to a hospital.*

Everybody in all the trucks turned backward to watch for the zombies. Justin's boy and girl leveled their .22 rifles along the railings of the truck bed. For several moments nothing happened. Justin started laying on his horn, and the other trucks joined in. It worked.

50

There were thick stands of trees on either side of the roadway they had just turned from. They couldn't see at first what was still following them. The intersection was still empty. Their eyes were fixed on the narrow gap where the road exited the trees.

"Like waiting on the floats at Mardi Gras," Patrick said leaning out his window. His wife tried shushing him.

"Yeah," Justin answered. "Parade from *hell*."

In the still that returned after the trumpeting of horns, they first heard a slapping sound. They saw it was a younger man in cargo shorts. One of his flip-flops was gone. The other was clinging to his left foot. The bare soul of his right foot and the remaining flip-flop slapped down hard against the asphalt as he staggered into view.

Justin honked a few more times. They watched as the young man swung his head towards them. Even Isherwood winced at the sight. The far side of his face was little more than a hole. The white of his cheekbone was clearly visible and his eye was gone.

It was a curious trick of sound that they were able to hear just the slapping feet of this zombie, because he had nearly an entire city of the dead behind him. Several zombies seemed to crash through the trees and into the shoulder at once. Some of the horde had apparently left the roadway and were slowed as they struggled through the underbrush. In moments, the lone zombie in cargo shorts had been joined by several hundred more.

Not long after the first wave of zombies stumbled into the intersection, they all had locked clouded and scratched eyes onto living flesh. They jerked their heads up the roadway and started moaning in the direction of the three trucks. Their rotting teeth and jaws started snapping at them, even though they were still another hundred yards or more away.

They could again see the gray fog spilling across the horizon in the distance behind them. It would all soon materialize into the staggering shapes of the walking dead if they waited long enough.

Isherwood leaped down from the bed of the truck and walked over to the driver's sides of the trucks. "Hey, do y'all mind if we scout ahead to the bridge. With you all minding the horde, I'll, I mean, Jerry and I will probably have time to clear out any stragglers on the bridge and hotwire and move vehicles out of the way. Then y'all will arrive at the head of the zombie snake and we'll lead it over the bridge together."

"Zombie snake, huh?" Justin chortled. "You idiot."

"So not keeping 'zombie parade'?" Patrick asked rhetorically. "But yeah, buddy," Patrick nodded, jutting out his bottom jaw, and confirming with his wife. "We can handle that."

"Yeah, sure," Justin smiled. "We got your back. Right, Chelsea?"

"Yea …," Chelsea started, before choking and having to swallow, having found that her throat had grown dry. "Yeah, Isherwood. We're good. It'll give the kids some good target practice. They've been hounding us since this thing started, you know."

"Keep them just in range, okay?" Isherwood asked. "Not too close. I'm not about to lose you guys now that we've just found each other, alright?"

They nodded to each other, letting their brave faces slip momentarily. "Patrick, you feel free to break off and warn us, if something changes. Wish to God we all had radios!"

"Your wish is my command," Justin laughed, slapping his forehead. "I should've mentioned these as soon as I saw you. My bad. Look, station four … okay, everybody?" Justin handed Isherwood two black rectangular radios, fully-charged with a shining green battery meter to prove it.

"*Dude*," Isherwood said, looking at the two radios in his hands as if they were gleaming bars of gold.

"Got one!" Patrick said, as Isherwood tried handing him a radio. "We've been working together for a few days now, once we realized we were probably all that was left of our neighbors."

"Patrick, what about Ms. Cathy?" Isherwood asked, knowing that Patrick had lived next door to his mom and dad. Patrick just shook his head and looked away.

"Okay, guys." Isherwood said, somberly stepping away from Patrick's beige Tahoe. "I'll be seeing you again in about twenty or thirty

52

minutes. We're gonna use the concrete divider separating the north and southbound lanes of the bridge to our advantage. We'll funnel them in, one long zombie snake, northbound. Then, we'll turn around southbound and haul butt, before they have a chance to turn around or spill over the divider. All that's left will be barricading the bridge behind us."

"Shouldn't we take them a little ways up US-61? You know, toward St. Francisville, before we turn back?" Justin asked.

"I thought about that, but there's only a grass median dividing US-61, not like the concrete divider that runs the three miles of approach bridges on the other side. I don't think we could get past them before they blocked the roadway. Besides, I think they'll scatter in time among all the rough terrain over there, making sort of a no man's land on the other side of the bridge, in case they've got the wrong sort of survivors over there."

Justin leaned over and opened his glove compartment. "I've got a map in here, somewhere. I'll line up some roads, just in case."

Isherwood initially tensed up, feeling uncomfortable with the loss of control. He relaxed by degrees as he realized his friend was right. "Isherwood?" Justin asked. "You looked far away there for a sec. You cool?"

"Yeah, yeah," Isherwood said, shaking his head to regain his focus. "No, that's a good idea. Thanks, buddy."

"Solid plan, brother," Patrick agreed. "Let's do it before flip-flop back there starts nibbling on my bumper."

CHAPTER SEVEN:
THE APPROACH

I t's a ghost town, Isherwood," Jerry said, as he pushed his gear shaft down into neutral. They had arrived at the foot of the bridge. "Looks like a good'un. This fool idea of yours might just work."

They got out of the truck, slamming the doors shut behind them. The sound echoed through the warm, humid air. There was only a slight note of rot drifting along with the wind across the open expanse of green fields and blue sky. Nothing, no businesses or buildings of any kind, had yet been built up around the bridge approaches. The bridge was still only a few years since completion. Isherwood had worked as a civil engineer on the project, though had left before its completion to teach for a stint at the local high school.

Upriver from the bridge beyond some stands of trees and more open green fields rose the smoke stacks of Big Cajun Power Plant. On a spring day such as this, one would expect to see white puffy clouds of vapor rising from the plant, but the plant had not been fully automated and lay dormant, likely never to run again. Rust would soon overtake the metal structure, eventually falling in on itself after wave upon wave of hot, humid Louisiana summers. The massive pile of coal that lay beyond it, however, could provide fuel for the newly-christened Kingdom of St.

Maryville for two generations or more to come. There were also ample supplies of timber to supplement it.

Beyond the river, on the St. Francisville side, lay a much more worrisome power plant, the *nuclear* power plant, River Bend Station. The enormity of the problem hadn't yet occurred to Isherwood, nor any of the others, who rarely, if ever, thought about what lay beyond the mile-wide Missisippi River at their backs.

"Look at *that*," Isherwood said. A radiant smile was spreading across his face. He was pointing to a stranded vehicle along the roadway. It was an eighteen wheeler. A crane stood perched above the trailer.

"That's no good, boy. It sits too high."

"What? What d'you mean?"

"The trailer. It won't block the bridge. See how it sits over three feet off the ground? They'll just crawl under it."

"Unless we tip it over," Isherwood frowned.

"Tip it?" Jerry howled. "Ain't got no chains, and this truck ain't powerful enough for that, neither. Maybe we could just shoot enough of them to clog it up when they start trying to squirm on under."

"Yeah, that could work. Or, if I drove it fast enough and turned the wheel fast enough at the last second, I could jack-knife it. It would wedge between the side of the bridge and the divider."

"You're crazy, kid. Might just shoot out the tires. It'll be sitting pretty low by then."

"Even so, that's still only one half of the bridge blocked off. Two of our trucks could finish the job, I bet, turned sideways and overlapping. Think you could hotwire *that* truck? Get it ready for the return trip?"

The older man muttered a string of curse words under his breath, but nonetheless cranked his truck back into drive.

*****

Jerry was standing beside the door to the cab of the eighteen-wheeler. He had asked that Isherwood cover him as he swung open the door to the cab. There was a bloody handprint running vertically down the cab's windshield. That pretty well satisfied them that there would be trouble within.

Sure enough, a ghoul came tumbling out of the cab as soon as Jerry swung the door open. It fell forward and out of the cab in a perfect nose dive, splitting into several desiccated pieces as it smashed into the concrete deck of the bridge. Its skull, remaining intact, was still staring up at Isherwood when Jerry crushed it under a boot heel.

"Thing must've mummified sitting in the heat of the cab all this time," Jerry observed grimly. "Blood must of all nearly evaporated out of it or something, but it was still coming. Stinkin' filth." Jerry gave the thing's skull another good kick. "Let me see if I can hotwire this thing."

"Might not have to," Isherwood said. He was rummaging through the remaining pieces of the zombie. "If this was the driver, the keys are still probably around here somewhere."

"Or still in the ignition!" Jerry said triumphantly. He gave the keys a tentative turn, expecting to hear the click-click of a dead battery. Instead, the huge engine roared to life. "Hot damn," the old man yelled above the heavy purr of the engine. He got out of the vehicle a few seconds later after checking out the rest of the cab. As he fell back to the ground with an arthritic wince, he said, "I'll just let her run for a little while, making sure the battery is good 'n charged."

"How much gas in the tank?" Isherwood asked before tapping the drum beneath the driver's seat.

"Almost half a tank. Plenty."

"Yeah, but if I try jack-knifing it, I might go up in smoke."

"Well, let's get it in position up top then." Jerry said. "We'll try the plug-the-holes-with-zombies plan."

From atop the bridge, Isherwood and Jerry could see practically all of the stretch of roadway leading from the last stoplight, nearly three miles of straight roadway cutting through the violent wash of green. They watched as the horde gradually darkened the roadway in the distance. Isherwood caught glimpses of his friend's two trucks as, ever so often, they came over a rise and the sun glinted off their windshields. Carrion birds were starting to swarm atop the horde, as well, marking the advance of the long and ragged gray snake.

"How much farther do you think?" Isherwood asked.

Jerry squinted into the distance. "Eh, I can't see too good. Can you tell if they've made it to the bridge over that railroad spur?"

"Why didn't I bring binoculars, or at least a rifle with a decent scope?" Isherwood complained as he stared intently into the distance. "Nah, I think they're just about to make it there, though."

"Probably another twenty minutes," Jerry said.

"Let's run down the road and see if we can grab an extra car, what d'ya say?"

"I don't know, kid," Jerry hesitated.

"One longish car could plug a big hole under that semi."

"Alright," Jerry grunted, rubbing his neck. "Let's go."

The old red truck growled its way back down the St. Maryville side of the bridge and curled away down underneath the approach bridge where the exit ramp met the River Road. They followed the road downriver, southward, toward a line of homes that gave way to a collection of sprawling neighborhoods called Waterloo.

"Look," Isherwood called out. "Let's stop there. There's even a four-wheeler." He was pointing toward a home at the end of a long driveway. Two cars were sitting in a carport. "Older-looking cars. Probably an older couple that died at home."

As they pulled into the driveway, they didn't see anything moving. Moments after slamming the doors, however, Isherwood heard tapping and scratching coming from inside the house. He was covering Jerry while he crawled under the dashboard of a late 90s Ford Taurus.

"There's a couple zombies in the house, tapping the windows at us, Uncle Jerry. No harm. I'm not gonna shoot them, but I thought you should know."

Jerry grumbled something resembling discomfort from under the dash. Isherwood kept moving and scanning the general area around the carport until the car's engine roared to life.

"How're we doing for time?" Jerry asked as he groped back to his feet, rubbing his back and knees.

"Just about ten minutes left," Isherwood answered.

"Good, let me see that," Jerry said putting his hand out for Isherwood's pistol. He handed it over without explanation, and watched as Jerry shoved the carport's screen door open and went inside the old zombie couple's home. He heard two quick shots and the zombies dropping to the floor. Jerry came barreling back out of the broken door, and handed Isherwood back his pistol, offering no explanation for his actions. Isherwood guessed that maybe Jerry had known the two people. They didn't seem much older than he was.

"Turns out we didn't need to hotwire the thing after all," Jerry said, still not looking at Isherwood, but holding up two sets of keys.

"A two for one special," Isherwood cried out happily, forgetting the solemnity of the moment.

"But let's get the Taurus first, anyway. It's longer than the Focus. These people sure loved their Fords."

*****

They spent the time they had left rearranging the few abandoned, or mostly abandoned vehicles, that were strewn around near the base of the bridge. Isherwood had realized the hole in his plan at some point and was hustling to correct it. They needed to funnel the horde into the northbound lane at the beginning of the concrete divider. If they didn't a fair number or even a very large number of zombies would be trapped in their exit corridor. They would be painting themselves into a corner.

Problem was, this couldn't be the place where they barricaded the southbound lane, because it was too far inland. Also, the barricades in both lanes needed to be side by side, if they were going to be effective. They had enough cars to make the funnel into the northbound corridor, but they would need even more to continue the barricade beside the eighteen-wheeler.

A minute or so later, they were back atop the bridge, and Isherwood was parking the Taurus behind the eighteen-wheeler. He put the keys between the visor and the soft cloth ceiling and closed the door, leaving it slightly ajar.

"No, you'll have to close the door," Jerry yelled over the din of his diesel engine. "Or else the dome and door lights will drain the battery. Roll the window down a little, instead."

Isherwood nodded and corrected his mistake, turning back to the old red truck. "Oh, my God," he said, frozen where he stood. Jerry turned around in the driver seat, looking back across the bed of his truck. "Ain't that a hell of a thing," he muttered.

As they watched, Justin and Patrick's vehicles were accelerating up the approach to the bridge. Maybe a quarter of a mile behind them, starting with a narrow trickle, like the snake's forked tongue, and quickly broadening to fifty or seventy-five abreast, the dead were following after them. It was an entire city of the dead. The gray, ragged snake of zombies was over a mile long, maybe two, reaching nearly all the way back to the last stoplight. The three or four hundred from Main Street had been joined by nearly three times that many from Hospital Road and maybe Parent Street, as well.

CHAPTER EIGHT: THE BRIDGE

The Audubon Bridge had been built without any great expectation of high traffic flow, at least not for several years, but it was needed as a hurricane evacuation route and as a third major artery connecting east and west sides of the Mississippi River between New Orleans and Natchez.

It was truly ironic that only now, at the end of all things, was it experiencing its first traffic jam.

The occupants of the three trucks had waited as long as they could at the top of the bridge, honking, catcalling, and carrying on, before they had jumped back in their vehicles and started their descent across the Mississippi River. As near as they could tell, the whole horde was staying on target.

"We must have nearly all of St. Maryville behind us," Justin's voice crackled over Isherwood's radio. "You've done good, you massive idiot, *click-shhh.*" The radio crackled with Justin's screechy laugh and then dissolved into static.

"Yeah, guys," Isherwood answered the radio, noting that the sun was starting to get low in the sky. "I think my plan might be working a little too well, unfortunately. That's too long a line of zombies for us to just double-back up the bridge, *click-shhh*."

"Sure you don't want to just stick to your original plan, Isherwood?" Patrick answered on the radio. "It may still work, *click-shhh*."

"Nah, I think an alternate route will be safer. Justin, didn't you say you were working on something? Over. *click-shhh*."

"Yeah, I gotcha back, buddy. Chelsea and I threw this together. Listen, then tell me what you think. We head south down US-61 a few miles until Country Road 126. We'll take a left there, and it'll take us straight up to Highway 966, which loops back onto US-61 about a half mile north of the road back to the bridge. What d'y'all think? We'd be leading those things so far from the bridge they'd never find their way back in sizeable numbers. They'd all scatter through the woods and hills up there, *click-shhh*."

Justin clicked back on a moment later. "Over. *click-shhh*."

"Yeah," Isherwood answered. "I think that's a solid plan, circling back around on the north side of 61. That should be good. *Real* good. Okay, here comes a tricky part. We're gonna need to consolidate vehicles. We've gotta leave something behind to finish blocking off the other lane up here. We could just leave it on the way back, but I think blocking off this other lane again is the smart play. We can't have these jerks clogging up our escape route. Patrick, would your family mind jumping in with us or Justin? Over. *click-shhh*."

There was a pause. It seemed Patrick must be discussing the question with his wife. "We gotta do what we gotta do. *click-shhh*."

There was radio silence for a while. They were all soon distracted by the nightmare that had begun to grow in their rearview mirrors. They could see the horde cresting over the smaller bridge behind them. Patrick was trying to distract his kids by pointing to the bridge. His wife had grown almost catatonic.

Isherwood called to them again on the radio, directing Patrick around the funnel and up the southbound lane and Justin up the northbound lane.

"Look kids," Patrick was saying. "Daddy's going the wrong way down the road."

"You can say that again," his wife mumbled under her breath.

Patrick made the sharp turn around the funnel that Isherwood and Jerry had made with the abandoned vehicles. Coming around the far side, a zombie suddenly appeared in front of them. The kids squealed in horror and his wife's eyes rolled back into her head. Patrick didn't mind, though. He was about to say goodbye to his vehicle forever, even though he had *just* finished paying it off. He hit the accelerator and the lone zombie thumped across the hood and up the windshield. They could hear it thudding against the roof and off the passenger side.

Patrick barely took his foot off the accelerator the rest of the way up the bridge. He screeched to a halt near the eighteen-wheeler as Isherwood had directed. He slid neatly into the last gap of the barricade, as the back end of his Tahoe fishtailed into position against the concrete divider. He sheared off just a millimeter or so of his bumper doing so.

"That was some James Bond crap right there," Isherwood was applauding as Patrick jumped out of the vehicle.

"Come on, lady. Kids," Jerry was saying. "There's room for y'all in the cab with me." Patrick and his wife handed their kids to Isherwood over the barrier. Everybody was soon over the wall. Patrick joined Isherwood in the bed of the truck. The caravan was soon on its way again. During the delay, however, the horde had narrowed the gap. Despite walking up an incline, the horde had closed to within a hundred yards.

They were soon watching the horde's progress through their rear view mirrors. The parents weren't even trying to stop their children from watching now. Despite the choke point made by the eighteen-wheeler and the Taurus, the zombie horde showed no signs of slowing. Amazingly, every last rotting corpse was staying confined to the northbound lanes of the bridge, thanks to Isherwood's funnel and the concrete barrier itself. If anything, a corpse now and then tumbled over the *side* of the bridge.

It was a sight to behold in the light of the setting sun. The northbound lanes were packed with corpses. A quarter mile of the corpses stretched down from the highest stretch of the bridge, and they were still coming.

"Don't start doubting yourself now, okay?" Patrick said, reading Isherwood's thoughts as they sat together in the bed of Jerry's truck. "There should be plenty of time to take this extra loop. Plus, we can take that opposite lane pretty fast on the way back. I don't remember seeing any, well maybe just one wreck. We might get by them before they're any wiser. Know what else? If we make good time, the last bit of the sunset will be shining in the zombies' eyes right as we're making our getaway back up the bridge. They might not even see us, only hear us, but by then we'll have passed them by. Let's just hope we don't need to use our headlights."

"Yeah. Yeah, I think you're right. Leading those things a bit farther from the bridge is the smart play, assuming the back roads aren't blocked. We'll get through it, come hell or high water."

"Wish you hadn't included that last part," Patrick added. "*Either* of those two last parts."

They spent the next thirty or so minutes traveling between five and ten miles per hour. The two trucks were basically huge carrots leading the zombies toward the intersection of LA-10 and US-61. When they finally arrived at the intersection, it was about 4:30pm. There was still plenty of daylight left. They stopped their vehicles in the intersection to allow the horde to get within spitting distance. If the horde began to break apart now, they might not be able to drive back through this intersection on their way out.

They did not have to wait long. The head of the zombie snake was less than a quarter of a mile behind them when they reached the intersection.

"How long do you think that thing is?" Isherwood asked over the radio. "Two miles maybe? *click-shhh.*"

"At least," Justin answered. "I thought it was gonna lengthen passing through the narrower roadway and that choke point by the eighteen wheeler, but somehow it thickened up and shortened. Over. *click-shhh.*"

"I'd say two miles almost to the dot," Patrick added. "You can almost count the green distance markers, *click-shhh.*" Isherwood took mental note that Patrick, since he was the local track coach, probably had a good idea of local distances.

The radios grew quiet as the hordes finally reached the end of the concrete divider. "All right, guys. Let's ease on down the highway some more. Over. *Click-shhh.*" The radio static was drowned out by the sound of their car horns honking.

Miraculously, an hour later, they were looking at the intersection from the opposite direction. They had led the horde a few miles down the highway before exiting quickly onto a side road and looping back around. They were able to drive at pretty much whatever speed they wanted once they had left the horde behind. There were some abandoned vehicles and zombies loitering around, but these were easily avoided or knocked aside. It took them less than a half hour to loop back around. By that time, the sun was setting, as Patrick had predicted.

Patrick shivered as he and Isherwood looked across the intersection of LA-10 and US-61. "Less than an hour ago, this place was packed with thousands of zombies. Can you believe that? And now, it's empty. Look down that road. No sign of them."

"That's really creepy, man. Let's not think about that just now, so long as the road back to the bridge looks clear. And it does."

Except the two trucks, there was no sign of life up or down the highway. Papers and trash were tossed around on the wind. The stoplights were black-eyed dead things waiting to rust. A few abandoned cars served only as wind blocks now. One perhaps held either a desiccated body or a trapped zombie, which couldn't be bothered to even moan at their passing.

"You can tell death passed this way, though," Isherwood said. "Wind or no wind, it still smells like it." Then, raising the radio, he said, "Let's get out of here, guys. Real quiet like. *Click-shhh.*"

The tires of the trucks crept along, declining to shout a last good bye to the former residents of their town. Slowly, they accelerated back up the southbound lane. This time, Justin took point in his blue Chevy truck. His kids were no longer shooting their .22s from the bed, but were buckled in. He slowed down to forty or so miles per hour once he realized how few of the zombies had been left behind by the main group. They were maybe a dozen all told. They could see many dozens more that the passing horde had flattened. Even now, the bones of the zombies must have softened, because very little remained of the trampled bodies. Justin later regretted never once firing his AR-15 into the crowd or at any zombies blocking his path. Their plan had worked to perfection.

When they reached the center of the bridge, the trucks parked just past the eighteen-wheeler and the Taurus. They all got out again, as they had when the zombies were still ascending the bridge. It was much quieter now.

"Can somebody help me get over this divider?" Jerry asked.

"Don't worry about it, Mister Jerry. I can maneuver the semi into place," Justin offered.

"Good," Isherwood nodded. "Can you shimmy the Taurus up under it, too?"

"No problem."

"I guess you'll be asking about Old Red, too, huh?" Jerry said with a tone more appropriate for a funeral. It was obvious that, even with all the vehicles already spanning the roadway, another one was still needed. "I suppose her time has finally come," he said.

"I suppose so, Uncle Jerry. I promise we'll make a shopping trip over to the dealership."

"Get me to the tractor dealership and we'll be more'n even," Jerry said.

"No problem. Deal. Can you and Patrick hold down the fort while I ride down the road real quick?"

"You bet, brother," Patrick nodded. "Hurry back."

When Justin's blue truck returned following a Ford Focus, the Tahoe and Old Red were pinned in, perfectly blocking all the southbound lanes. Justin, too, had rammed the semi in sideways as far as could, and was working on squeezing the Taurus underneath the trailer, as well. The roof was beginning to collapse in, as he pushed farther and farther under the eighteen-wheeler. "This is sorta fun!" Justin called out, laughing his screechy laugh. "National Lampoon's made this look *a lot* easier, though."

"Alright, buddy," Isherwood called over from the southbound lane. "Come help us flip over these trucks. We've got four grown men and two ladies. I think we can do it. That little Focus might help finish the job, either by pushing or as a buttress when it's all done."

"Dang," Justin called out from atop the concrete barrier. "There's *still* no sign of 'em. We can just sit back and enjoy the sunset if we want. Isherwood, you idiot, you're a genius."

In the end, they decided to slide the Focus where the two trucks met in the middle to prevent the onrush of zombies from pivoting the vehicles and making a small gap. They also stopped short of flipping the Focus, leaving it in good working order with the keys under the visor in case they needed a getaway vehicle someday.

By about six, the job was finished. Justin took another look over their blockades, and spotted an oncoming group of zombies. "Here come the hole pluggers!" He announced.

"Northbound or southbound?" Isherwood asked.

"A little bit of both," Justin answered, but nobody knew if that was good or bad. "Good for plugging holes, anyway," Justin concluded.

A few moments later, Isherwood was calling out to one of the zombies. "Okay, ugly. That's right. Come at me across the hood. Come on. That's good right there." *Blam.* "Alright, next up. Come crawl up on this guy's carcass. That's right." *Blam.*

"Just like building with Lincoln logs, am I right?" Justin called out as he slowly wedged bodies into gaps here and there.

After another couple of minutes, Isherwood called out. "Back off, guys. Let's see if any of them can get through. We can overdo this, if were not careful. Like at Masada."

"I heard you say 'at Tostada' under your breath, man." Patrick said, calling Isherwood out. "Now, *you know*, nobody has any idea what you're talking about. That's just silly, bro. And I'm really hungry, besides. Okay?"

"Nevermind," Isherwood said, brushing off the comment. "I think she's holding. I haven't heard old Uncle Jerry's truck even budge. Let's get out of here ASAP, okay? That's good enough for a day's work *and* it's still light out."

They rode back to the church in Justin's blue Chevy. They packed the women, kids, and Jerry inside the cab, while Isherwood, Justin, and Patrick rode guns out in the bed. The sun was just setting as they rolled back onto Main Street. There were still zombie stragglers here and there, but the streets were mostly empty.

"I want to thank you, buddy, for a good day." Patrick took Isherwood by the shoulder. "It's only really been two weeks or so, but I felt like I'd never have another one of those again."

"Yeah, hope was growing *real* thin at our house," Justin added. "You and your idiot megaphone might've come along at the last possible second."

Isherwood was just shaking his head. "I can't believe of all the people to run into, it was you guys. I'm sorry to admit it, but I didn't even think about passing by your subdivision. I guess I'd just locked away all hope of specific people, let alone friends, surviving. I mean, seriously? That's incredible. You know what it means? You two, your young families, your skills, your smarts – we can start to *rebuild*. We might just pull it all off, after all."

"What d'you mean, survival? A farm? What?" Patrick asked.

"No, man." Isherwood answered. The sunset was twinkling in his eyes. "True blue civilization. Like Monsignor said, a *kingdom*."

"The name could use a little work, maybe an empire or principality or something," Justin waxed on. "Not duchy, of course. *Definitely* not grand duchy, sounds like a royal crap. But I like where you're going with this."

CHAPTER NINE: STARTER RAIDS

"You know, Smithy," Sara said to her husband, encircling him with her slender arm. It was the morning after Isherwood had found Justin and Patrick's families and cleansed the town of the hordes.

After their morning coffee, Sara and Isherwood had found a metal ladder which led up from the office behind the church's choir loft. It led up to a hole in the ceiling which opened into the bell tower. From there, they were able to survey all of downtown St. Maryville and were at eye level with the clock tower of the Parish Courthouse four blocks east on Main Street. The town looked still and gray. Newspapers and trash fluttered across Main Street and the parking lot beside City Hall. There were still pockets of movement here and there, as the dead shambled aimlessly about, sometimes chasing the odd rat or river vermin. The ducks, what was left of them, were returning to the piers and river landings. The great, long crescent of False River stretched out before them and the Mississippi stretched endlessly in either direction before them.

"If you make a raid on Wal-Mart today," Sara continued, smiling up at her husband. "You could pick me up a bowfishing set."

Her husband looked up from surveying the town at his feet. "Don't you think False River's a little murky for that? Besides, we shouldn't risk fishing just yet with still so many of those creeps walking around."

Sara smiled mischievously. "Oh no, honey. I was thinking I'd go bowfishing for zombies."

"Huh?" Isherwood looked down at her in confusion.

"Don't you get it? I'm honestly surprised you hadn't thought of it yet. Your head's always so full of ideas. You're planning on drawing the remaining zombies to the church, aren't you? Like our little chicken feeder-trap back on Delaware Avenue. We can use spears to poke their little skulls far enough away to keep them from piling up against the fence –"

"Well, yeah, but we'll probably just start hauling them off to a burn pile."

"Sure, but – just listen – I'm limited on how much I can use my bow from inside the fence because of the wasted arrows, right?"

"Ohhh, gotcha."

"I knew you would." She laughed girlishly and squeezed him tighter. "If my brothers can haul in six hundred pound alligator gar with the line on those bowfishing arrows, I just know I could get my arrows back. No waste."

"I love it! That's an awesome idea, Sara," Isherwood said, squeezing his wife tighter. "I love it when you get all zombie killer on me – and preventing waste, too? You're a geek's dream come true."

"Look at that little guy. He's waving at us." Sara pointed down at a zombie that had spotted their bell tower perch from the street below. It was reaching for them and moaning.

Isherwood looked from the lone zombie that had spotted them, and his eyes began darting from zombie to zombie still shambling along Main Street and the side streets. A burst of caffeine made his heart flutter. "It's time I got back to work," he told his wife.

Sara smiled bittersweetly. "You've gone back in your man cave, haven't you?" She asked, but it wasn't really a question.

*****

"Listen," Isherwood was addressing the dining room of the rectory. The number of survivors had quickly outstripped the size of the dining room table. "I know it makes sense – a lot of sense – to start raiding places right here around us first. And it's true – we need to bring in all the perishables at Langlois' grocery ASAP and start canning and preserving them. But I really think we need to make a raid on Wal-Mart. It's pretty much the *only* source of guns and ammo in this whole area, short of stashes in private homes, *and* we need to at least check out what effect we've had on the population of zombies on Hospital Road."

"Come on, buster." Justin was smiling sarcastically. Isherwood could see he was getting ready to unload one of his screechy howls of laughter. "We know you just want to go on a shopping spree in the gun department. Come on, admit it."

Isherwood couldn't help but smile, despite himself. Everybody else broke out into laughter. It was a great sound to hear, and increasingly rare in these last days. It was even better to hear such a group laughing, Isherwood thought darkly to himself, because the volume helped drown out Justin's screeching.

"Okay! I'll admit it," Isherwood said, also trying to return order to the group. "But even so – we don't know how much time we have before something happens to Wal-Mart's supplies. It may already be heavily picked over. I'm also worried about fire breaking out along Hospital Road. Plus, it will be target number one for other raiding parties, if there any others. *And –*"

"Whoa! Down boy," Patrick said. "You've already convinced us, man."

"I agree," said Monsignor, seated at the head of the table. "Besides, I'm running short on .308 centerfire bullets for my Winchester. I think I've got only two."

71

"And I've already told you what I could do with a bowfishing bow and arrow set," Sara added. "I doubt the fishing equipment will be picked over."

"You know," said Patrick. "There's even a chance – I heard a rumor when everything was going down the tubes. I think they locked up Wal-Mart because of all the looting. If we're gonna raid that sucker, we're gonna need bolt-cutters for sure."

"Probably a blow torch, too," Aunt Tad said, looking at Jerry.

"What?" Jerry grumbled, as people started looking at him. "I can't hear half the things you people are saying."

"Blow torch!" Tad said over-enunciating so Jerry could hear. "To get into *Wal-Mart*!"

"Oh yeah," Jerry nodded agreeably. "Got a whole kit back in my shed. Acetylene tanks, too."

"We could swing by Delaware Ave easy," Isherwood nodded.

"And if y'all are talking raids on Wam-a-lart and the car dealerships," Jerry went on. "We oughtta be talking about a trip to John Deere, too. We need to get plantin' now. Plenty of dirt to till inside this fence, but ain't nobody gonna wanna do it by hand."

"Too many top priorities!" Isherwood said, shaking his head. "Well, sounds like we're gonna need a starter raid for supplies before we can get into Wal-Mart after all. If we're going back to Delaware Avenue for Jerry's torch, might as well clear the perishables out Langlois grocery, too."

"Better get all the canning jars they have, too, *especially* quart size and bigger," Gran added. "Sounds like Tad and I are going to have a lot to do, but we'll get these new ladies, Chelsea and Denise, and the kids to help us, too. We'll make short work of it."

*****

The younger men and Jerry again left the women and children inside the church grounds, while they rode down Main Street to Langlois' grocery. Monsignor again took up his rifle perch on the second floor of the rectory. Gran and Tad busied themselves with mapping out the eastern edge of the church yards into a large vegetable garden. They planned to leave the back of the church grounds, the ten or so acres of open land on the north side, for crops that needed more space like corn and potatoes.

"Things must've gone down even faster than I realized," Isherwood said, staring at the locked sliding glass door of Langlois' corner grocery. They had parked along the sidewalk outside the grocery store, and were fanning out around the store, one quadrant at a time, clearing out the surrounding houses, yards, and side streets.

Main Street continued past Langlois' grocery and along the northern bank of False River until it ran into Waterloo, around the corner of which they had snagged the two cars the day before. For the next mile or so, Main Street was still lined with white houses flying American flags from white porches surrounded by neat green lawns, azalea bushes, and white picket fences. There were several sprawling plantations along the way, as well. At the end of the line but still before Waterloo, after the houses again gave way to green pastures and pecan orchards, there was Wickcliffe Plantation, Isherwood's ancestral home.

"Why you say that?" Patrick asked.

"Because the sliding glass door isn't smashed and there's no sign that anybody even tried to force it open," Isherwood answered.

"Maybe they all went through the back door like you," Justin added.

"I guess, but it seemed like I was the only one coming and going," Isherwood answered. "By the way, the fresh fruits and vegetables aisle might be a scary sight."

Patrick looked at him with a wry grin. "I just popped a zombie in the face, and its eyeball exploded back on me. Some of that fetid eye juice almost got in my mouth, too! And you're telling me rotting cabbages are gonna scare me?"

Isherwood didn't even try to respond. He was doubled over laughing. Patrick was chuckling, too. "Alright, guys," Justin said, smiling. "Let's get on with it. This whole block only had about a dozen zombies. Looks like Uncle Jerry's going on ahead without us, anyway."

Jerry was trying to pry the sliding door open with a crow bar and cursing a blue streak.

"Hey, Uncle Jerry." Isherwood tapped him on the shoulder. "Let's just go in the back entrance to keep this door intact."

"Fine," Jerry said, letting the crowbar rattle noisily to the ground. "I was about to smash this stupid glass in – glad you stopped me."

The main section of the grocery store was a cinder block building without windows. Without electricity, it was a dark and dank place.

Isherwood led them into the store through the back. The door was a standard lever-entrance steel door. They just had to push on it to open it. It stood behind a little fence, though, so it would be odd for a zombie to accidentally run into it – odder still, for it to stay open long enough for more than one to slink through.

"I think the backup generators must have kicked in daily for a while until the gasoline gave out," Isherwood explained, "Because the freezers were still working for a long time after the electricity gave out. If the meat is still cool in the back, I say we take as much as we can. The women can cut it into chunks and can it. What d'you think, Uncle?"

"We'll smell it fast if the meat's spoiled. Otherwise, it's just aging the beef. A good freezer – like they got in here – will keep the cool for a long time after shutting down."

They could hear Justin's stomach start to growl. "I was just starting to think about that sound hamburgers make when you throw them on a grill," he explained.

"The problem'll be butcherin' without those saws they got." Jerry was still talking out loud as they went about checking and clearing the store for zombies.

"Sonofa! Whoa!" Patrick called out, before a quick *BLAM! BLAM!* The pistol shot was near-deafening in the closed space.

"You okay, Patty O'Hooligan?" Isherwood asked.

"I'm fine," he answered from somewhere near the front corner of the store near the glass door. "The thing was probably drawn to the sound of Uncle's crowbar from before. Can somebody help me drag this thing outta here? *Don't want to draw any antsies!*" Patrick finished his request with an effeminate flair.

"Just unlock the sliding glass door and toss that thing into the bushes," Justin offered. "Beats dragging that bag of filth back through the whole store."

"An excellent idea, sire," Patrick sniveled jokingly, and busied about like a hunchback or Igor. Isherwood noted that the fear of the last days was beginning to slough off his friends, as Patrick grew sillier and Justin more focused. They had always balanced each other, as long as he had known them.

Isherwood heard Jerry pulling out the pin and yanking on the lever of the large walk-in freezer they had passed when entering the store. *"Burrr!"* Jerry yelled from inside. "Oh yeah, this'll do just fine. Just fine, indeed!" Isherwood heard him saying to himself as he hurried to the back to join him.

"Don't open the door too wide," Jerry barked at Isherwood.

Patrick and Justin followed them into the freezer after another minute. Justin had holstered his pistol, trading it for a bag of chips and a can of bean dip.

"You didn't waste any time," Isherwood teased him.

"Mmm," he gurgled from a packed mouth. He mumbled out another sentence, sloshing around the bean and chip paste.

"What'd he say?" Isherwood asked.

"I think he said 'The taste of civilization,'" Patrick answered. "Gross."

"Eat up," Jerry said from inside the freezer. "It's gonna take every ounce of meat we got to move this meat." Inside the long freezer, which ran the entire length of the back of the store, they stared in wonder at a long rack holding about twenty sides of beef from frosted steel hangars. Shelves ran along either side filled with hundreds and hundreds of pounds of deli meat, whole chickens, hams, prepared dinners, stacks of bacon, boxes and boxes of meat paddies and sausage, as well as every kind of seafood imaginable.

"We're gonna need *a lot* of jars." Justin mumbled from a slack jaw.

"And salt." Jerry nodded.

"Yup," Isherwood said. "Dehydration is out for now in this humidity."

"Does this mean we'll need to take a visit to the car lot?" Patrick said, wiggling his eyebrows. "Remember, I'm still out a Tahoe."

"That gives me an idea," Isherwood said with widening eyes.

"I'm sure it does," Justin grumbled with a mouth still sloshing with bean dip.

CHAPTER TEN:
NO FREE MEALS

"Before we get too far ahead of ourselves," Isherwood told the others. "I'm gonna scout out our exit strategy." There was already an old zombie hag raking a bony fingertip against the sliding glass door.

They had closed the freezer door for now and had filled up shopping carts with all the remaining uncanned fruit and vegetables, as well as all the canning jars the store had.

"Let's just roll it all back in the carts," Patrick argued. "There's not room enough for it all in the bed of Justin's truck."

They heard the door scrape open, as Isherwood left to make a quick scan around the building. However, the door slammed closed almost immediately upon opening. They heard Isherwood cursing under his breath as he came back to the main part of the store. "Surprise! We're surrounded."

"How the hell?" Justin threw up his hands. "There weren't any around, except that one chick at the door – " He stopped suddenly, still pointing at the door.

"Like rats," Jerry cursed.

"It appears our little friend at the door brought her whole sewing circle along, too." Isherwood remarked grimly. "Either door, we're busting in on a group of six or more in close quarters."

"Can you get up on the roof of this place?" Justin asked. "If they're close enough, we'll just poke some holes in their heads. If not, we'll use the guns. No problem, right?"

"Yeah, yeah. That makes sense. I think I saw a ladder by the deli meat slicer – it should lead up to the roof."

Jerry elected to stay inside the store with his feet flat on the ground, thank you very much.

"Suit yourself," Justin said, as he wriggled through the small opening in the roof, following Isherwood and Patrick. Before climbing up himself, he lifted a couple frog gigging poles up through the hole and a sledge hammer for good measure.

The sun was almost directly overhead now. The morning had drained away quickly. "Luckily," Isherwood said, peering over the side of the building, "they're just bunched at the two doors. I can't believe none of them pushed open the back door."

"Gig'em," Patrick winked at Isherwood, as he leaned over the three foot or so of wall that rose above the tarred flat roof. The top of the wall was at most eight feet higher than the heads of the zombies. "Uh, hold my feet, okay? They're farther down than I thought they'd be."

"*Bam!*" Patrick said, making his own sound effects, as he plunged the metal-tipped wooden pole into the skull of one of the zombies below. There was an odd stretch of silence from Patrick, interrupted by the moans of the dead below that had taken notice of the man hanging over the side of the building. "Dang, it's still going. I know I pierced the skull."

"Probably didn't do enough damage to the brain. Give it another whack."

"*Bam!*" Patrick said again. "*Bam! Bam!* Fourth time's the charm." He cheered as he pulled himself back over the wall. "Wow," he said, catching his breath.

"Good job, Bam Bam," Justin said, taking the second pole and handing it to Isherwood. "Your turn, Pebbles."

After a few more rounds of this with Isherwood and Patrick taking turns and Justin holding their feet, there was a mound of corpses piled up against the exterior wall. It had been easier going as the zombies mounded up on each other, getting closer and closer to the top of the wall.

"There's that one last short booger that not even Isherwood's long arms can reach," Justin observed. "Distract him with the pole for a sec, okay?" He asked Patrick, and walked back over to the roof access hatch they had crawled through. "Hey, Uncle!" he called down. Moments later, Jerry opened the door and dispatched the diminutive zombie with a meat tenderizer.

They climbed back down from the roof and took care of the old hags' sewing circle from street level. Next, they rattled their shopping carts out the back door, not really caring what might hear the noisy baskets. They loaded what they could into the bed of the truck for Jerry to drive back, and decided to wheel back the rest in the buggies. Justin, for his part, mounted the two frog gigging poles through the front of his cart like devil horns.

It was only a few blocks back to the church, so they decided to drop off their groceries and then go back to Delaware Avenue for Jerry's welding supplies. There were a few stray zombies wandering around in front of the courthouse and Raymond's pharmacy, which were easy enough to take care of as they passed. Isherwood thought he saw Patrick kill Raymond the pharmacist, himself, but Patrick didn't recognize him from the commercials.

"Dangit," Justin cursed, as they passed Ma Mama's Restaurant. "Glad I brought these giggin' poles. Ain't no free meals in the zombie apocalypse."

The shopping carts rattled to a stop a block from the church, and the blue Chevy truck stopped behind them. There at least thirty zombies banging against the fence and blocking the south gates of the church.

*****

"Guys, we better conserve ammo until we can get to Wal-Mart," Isherwood said, holstering his pistol. "Besides, the guns will only draw more zeds."

"Wish they weren't blocking the road," Justin grumbled, pulling the frog gigging sticks out of his shopping cart. "We could just peg their heads with these from inside the fences."

Isherwood walked back to the truck, and pulled a baseball bat from the bed. "If we just stand our ground, they should only come three or so at a time. Hey, Uncle Jerry – why don't you stay in the truck and watch our backs, okay?"

"Want a gigging pole?" Justin asked Patrick.

"Nah, takes too many holes to bring 'em down. I'm gonna use this." Patrick drew out the six-pound mini-sledge hammer out of the shopping cart like Excalibur.

"Not if you knock 'em – POW – right in the eye. Besides, Donatello was my favorite ninja turtle," Justin smiled boyishly, slinging around one of the sticks. "What I wouldn't give for a lightsaber, though."

"You'd just slice off your own head," Isherwood said, planting his feet and getting into his Ted Williams batting stance, while he twisted the Louisville Slugger in his grip. He took a few practice swings.

"Well, at least the wound would be cauterized, idiot," Justin popped back. There were lined up with Isherwood to the left, because he could switch hit, Patrick in the center, and Justin to the far right. They kept buildings to either side of them to keep from getting too spread out and to protect their flanks. The shopping carts stood between them and the truck, and Jerry angled the truck into place long-ways behind them to protect their rear.

"Good point," Isherwood agreed. "Here they come!" It happened that the first zombie, though it was angling for Patrick, stumbled instead over to Isherwood. Isherwood pivoted on his back foot to swing the bat right-handed, and yelled, "Got it!"

Thwack! Isherwood swung the bat, hitting the zombie about an inch behind its right eyebrow. The skull collapsed inward, crushing what was left of the frontal cortex.

"Nice," Patrick nodded. "Maybe a double?"

The three men didn't say much more as they got down to business. Justin took on the next zombie. He only managed glancing blows scraping against the thick bone around the brow. Then, he hit pay dirt. He planted his foot behind him so that he was perpendicular to his target. He bent his knees, lowering his center of gravity, and exploded forward. He thrust the pole straight into the zombie's eye socket, and there was an audible clink as the metal tip clanged against the back of the skull. Justin pulled backward quickly, as well, in one fluid motion.

"Nice one," Isherwood called out.

"Watch out for the eye juices," Patrick added, as he whirled the mini-sledge down through a zombie skullcap. "You see that? Broke straight through the back of the skull, and the skin is *unbroken*. Clean kill, no contaminants, no juices."

"Thanks, Danny Tanner," Justin said as he reared back, readying to thrust his gigging pole. "Wwwwake *up!* San Francisco," he said, again thrusting the pole straight back into the skull.

"Idiot," Isherwood laughed. He took a moment to wipe his mouth on his sleeve before pushing a zombie backward with the top of his bat. He again squared up, waiting for it to regain its balance and swung as its head slumped forward into the strike zone.

It was all over in less than ten minutes. Isherwood wiped the gore from the face of his Timex. "Gah, 2pm. We better hurry if we're gonna unload and make it back to Delaware Ave for the torch *and* pick up what's left of my chickens."

"Well, let's get going," Jerry barked. "A man can get old sitting in a truck all day."

"Wait – wasn't he our age when we left the grocery store?" Justin whispered to Patrick as they reclaimed their shopping carts, chunking their weapons into the child seats.

81

CHAPTER ELEVEN: WAL-MARTIANS

"We're out of almost every type of ammo except 9mm," Sara remarked over coffee the next morning. "It's now or never." The Smiths, Gran, and Monsignor were all gathered again for morning coffee.

"I've got nothing at all left for my rifle," Monsignor nodded.

"Oh, don't you worry," Isherwood shook his head. "Today is the day. Come hell or high water."

"You gotta stop using that phrase, Smith," Sara said, putting down her coffee a little too hard.

"Hell's come," Monsignor agreed. "It's at the gates."

There came a rumbling of feet above their heads, as the chandelier above the dining table twinkled a little. "Oh!" Gran smiled, "sounds like somebody's awake."

"And everyone else soon will be," Aunt Lizzy grumbled from under her blankets in the side parlor.

"That's just as well," Gran sighed. "Lots of work for us to do today here on the home front. Those vegetables won't wash, peel, and can themselves."

The blankets were rising from the couch in the side parlor, as though Nosferatu lay beneath them. The blankets hung for a moment and then fell gradually from Lizzy's face. "All right, Rosie. I'm up. I'm up."

"That's good to hear," Tad clapped as she rounded the staircase, just emerging from the larger parlor and striding joyously into the dining room. "We've got lots of work to do today, washing, peeling, and canning all those vegetables!"

"*My* God. They're in stereo," Lizzy wailed, falling back down onto the side parlor couch.

The quick pitter-pat of little feet rumbled down the stairs and across the wood floors into the dining room. They all watched as the little girl disappeared under the dining room table and reappeared on the other side of the table, scrambling onto a dining room chair. She plopped herself down on the cushion and looked around the table with clenched teeth and mounting excitement. "Dee-dee's awake! Dee-dee's awake! It's canning day today? It's my buft-day!" And then she popped her thumb into her mouth.

As quickly as she had come, she was sliding back down off the chair. She reappeared under the dining room table at Monsignor's lap, and began climbing up and over the old man's knees. "You snuckle me? Mozeener, you snuckle me? Okay? Thanks," the little girl said, as she snuggled into Monsignor's lap.

*****

About an hour or so later, Isherwood, Justin, and Patrick found themselves right back where they started – along Major Parkway, right outside the entrance to what used to be their subdivision.

"I'd love to just honk the horn, and see what numbers come stumbling our way," Isherwood said, as the blue Chevy sat idling in the intersection of the Wal-Mart road and Major Parkway. They were between the unfinished nursing home and the Washburn building. Several thousand feet of sugar cane still stood between them and the back of the Super Wal-Mart, and just a bit farther, Hospital Road.

"But quiet's better. This time," Jerry answered from the driver's seat.

"Okay, so here's the plan. One more time." Isherwood turned to face the others in the back seat. "We go in through the Tire & Lube Entrance. I don't think there's a metal safety door covering that door. All the rest have those garage door-like security grills, which we'll need Uncle Jerry and his blow torch to cut through. If we can get in through the auto repair door, we roll up the door to one of their maintenance bays and stash the truck in there. If not, we'll cut open one of the delivery doors along the backside to keep out of view of Hospital Road and what's left along it."

Patrick clicked on the radio. "Denise, you there? We're back on Major Parkway about to head in to Wal-Mart. *Click-shhhh.*"

"Uncle Jerry, you got your radio?" Isherwood asked. Jerry picked up the radio from the dash and flipped it on, all without saying a word.

"Denise? Over?" Patrick repeated.

"I thought you said they were good for over five miles," Isherwood complained.

"Eh, maybe five miles of open water, but we—"

"Patrick? We're here. *Click-shhhh,*" Denise answered.

Patrick clicked back. "Good. Thanks, love. Remember, please don't use the radio unless it's an emergency. And please don't have an emergency, okay? Love you all."

Another five minutes passed and the blue Chevy was turning into the back entrance of the Wal-Mart. They had only encountered two stray zombies along the side road, and Jerry had been able to run both down with the truck, slowing them down considerably. Isherwood made a mental note that they would need to start upgrading the vehicles for running over zombies without clogging up the works, reinforcing the windows, roof turrets – he had to stop himself, as his mind starting racing with new ideas to distract himself from his present anxiety.

Isherwood turned his attention to the present, trying to lock onto something that would scare him enough to keep focused. He noticed more zombies tripping across the furrows of the sugar cane fields. He thanked God the sugar cane wasn't yet taller than the heads of the zombies, or there would be no telling how many zombies lay between them and their way out. He thought darkly that it would be the zombie apocalypse version of *Field of Dreams*.

As they turned into the alleyway along the back of the store, they saw another three or four zombies staggering around and slowly turning in their direction. Uncle Jerry took careful aim, choosing to run them down and over with the left side of the truck.

Justin was giggling in the back seat, as Jerry made short work of the zombies. "It's kinda like Whack-a-Mole, it'nt it?" He laughed, as Isherwood turned back to look at him. Isherwood shook his head in mock disdain, and noticed that Jerry was smiling as he drove. *Good opportunity for stress relief*, Isherwood thought to himself. He was starting to pay more attention to the morale of their group, as he slowly shouldered some leadership of the group. Obviously, he wanted Monsignor to be the leader – the priest would always be *his* leader – but maybe he could be sort of a Chief of Operations. He had plenty of ideas, anyway. *And maybe that's all it takes sometimes*, he concluded, feeling somewhat naïve in his assessment.

Isherwood tightened the grip on the axe he was holding, as they prepared to round the back corner of Wal-Mart turning into the small parking lot adjacent to the Tire & Lube department. "Go slow, okay, Uncle Jerry?" Isherwood could feel everyone tensing up, as well. "There," he pointed. "Y'all see that nursing home or whatever it is? That's what I'm worried about, besides zeds still coming from Hospital Road, whatever's in the parking lot, and whatever's inside. Don't forget we've got that place at our backs."

"Gah, I never realized this city was so full of nursing homes," Justin complained.

"Wheelchair zombies," Patrick laughed nervously.

As they finished talking, the truck rounded the corner. Jerry slowed to a stop for a moment. There was nothing. No zombies at all that they could see. "Wow." Isherwood felt his heart leap in his chest. "Awesome." He asked Jerry to come forward a little farther, so the truck would be hidden from view from the back side of the store. "Come on, guys. Let's see if we can get that door open, so we don't have to mess with the security grills and the blow torch."

The three younger men slid out of the cab, leaving Jerry to man the getaway truck. The wind was blowing east, back the way they had come, and so hopefully was carrying the truck's engine noises away into the cane fields. There was a long chain link fence behind the Wal-Mart, as well as a drainage servitude that would keep at bay any zombies coming at them from the cane fields.

They hurried to an exterior entrance that was protected by a doorless concrete wall. It was likely intended as sort of a rain porch, but it was especially helpful in the current situation to conceal their movements and noise as they pried at the steel entrance. The doors to the maintenance bays stood closed, as had been expected. Patrick ran over to check them on the off chance they weren't locked, but he returned shortly shaking his head.

"Okay, guys. Like we practiced. About here look right?" Isherwood asked the other two, as he put his waist against the door and marked a spot with a Sharpie. Patrick and Justin nodded quietly. "Okay. Justin, you got my umbrella? Okay, good. Stand back while I swing the axe. It's pretty tight in this little porch-thing." Isherwood took a practice swing of the axe, leveling it at the black mark on the steel door. He was actually pretty practiced with an axe, though he preferred his Louisville Slugger for close combat. He had attended a college where the majority of the second half of the Fall Semester was spent chopping down woods to provide logs for a massive bonfire. But, he was not practiced at being quiet while he swung an axe. He took out the saint medal from around his neck and kissed it. "Ready? Here goes."

Keeping his eye on the mark, Isherwood reared back, fully extending. As he swung, he let his right hand slide down along the smooth wood of the axe handle until it came to rest atop his left. RIP-*KA-RONGGG*. The door reverberated with the impact as axe head sank into the steel, tearing open a four-inch or so gap straight through the door.

"Okay, try the umbrella." Justin tried pushing the curved wooden handle of Isherwood's umbrella through the gap. The gap was long enough. That was good.

But Justin shook his head. "Wider," he said.

"See anything?" Isherwood said to Patrick, who was watching the front corner of the building. They were hidden behind the tall, outdoor storage area of the Outdoors department, but they knew little would cover the sound of the axe blows.

"Alright. Get back. *Headache*," Isherwood called out in a whisper as he swung the axe again.

Justin again tried pushing the handle of the umbrella through the torn steel. This time, after a little wiggling, it slid through.

"Yes!" Isherwood whispered loudly and nodded to Justin. Justin rotated the shaft of the umbrella ninety degrees, so that the handle of the umbrella was now pointing down on the inside of the other side of the door. "Pull it," Isherwood smiled.

They heard the soft screech of metal, as the panic bar clanged and collapsed on the other side of the door. The door popped open.

Justin smiled, still holding the umbrella. "You idiot," he added, admiring Isherwood's idea. "You stupid idiot. That was awesome."

"Thanks, buddy." Isherwood winked. "Hand me my umbrella, would'ya?"

"Just in case there's a crap storm in Zombieland, right buddy?" Patrick laughed. He turned back to Jerry in the truck and gave him a thumbs up, as the three men slipped inside the door. None of them took notice of the small trickle of zombies that had begun stumbling around the corner of the vertical stacks of compost and potting soil outside the gardening section.

*****

The three men stepped inside the darkened automotive department of the Super Wal-Mart. "Thank God," Patrick said looking up to the ceiling. "I thought I remembered there being sky lights. Otherwise, it'd be dark as pitch in here."

"Yeah, but look at *that*," Justin swung a thumb behind him to the security grill that was drawn down, separating the automotive check-out area from the rest of the store.

"Crap-tastical," Patrick said, letting his head drop to his chest.

"No, nah," Isherwood said.

"Poor guy's in denial," Justin informed Patrick with mock sympathy.

"No," Isherwood said again. "I mean this might be a blessing in disguise. We don't have to worry about those creeps jumping us until after we've got Uncle Jerry and the truck inside. Come on," he said, knocking loudly on the linoleum countertop beside a credit card reader. "Justin, will you look for a manual override lever or chain or something to get one of those bay doors open? Don't want to leave Uncle out there. He won't be able to see anything coming until ten yards or less, poor guy."

Isherwood and Patrick swept first the maintenance bays, while Justin started rummaging around. Leaving Justin, they hopped back over the check-out counter to sweep the back bay where the tall stacks of tires and other equipment stood.

Isherwood had left his umbrella on the checkout counter, but was still holding the axe. They were all keeping their pistols holstered until they got Jerry's truck inside.

Patrick thought Isherwood was still at his side, and so, at first, didn't notice the dark shape lunging at him from the shadows. He dodged out of the way as the thing lunged at him. They both went sprawling onto the smooth, cold painted concrete floor. Patrick knocked into a portable battery charger on his way down that wobbled a bit and then steadied itself, like one of those Bozo the clown inflatable punching bags. The zombie, however, bore no resemblance to the clown except for the sickly white skin, absent of color as the corpse's blood had long drained into its lower extremities. The thing reached for Patrick's heel with its grease-stained fingers, as Patrick groped blindly in the half-light for his mini-sledge. In his panic, he had forgotten the pistol still holstered at his hip.

The thing had his ankle, and Patrick knew with paralyzing fear that teeth would soon close around his Achilles.

The thing's grip around Patrick's heel suddenly relaxed as a terrible scraping sound echoed across the cavernous back maintenance bay. Sparks flew up from the floor, momentarily illuminating a face full of malice. It was Isherwood. His axe had come down hard on the concrete floor, passing through the rotting corpse smoothly and severing the zombie's head right at the first cervical vertebrae.

Isherwood let the axe drag back to him, scraping against the floor, as he bent over panting. He put his hand to his head. "Man, something just took over me. Thought I had lost you," he said between pants.

Before Patrick could thank Isherwood, he was scrambling to his feet at the sound of Justin calling to them for help.

"What the heck, man?" Patrick called over to Justin when he and Isherwood came running into the main maintenance bay. "I thought you were in actual trouble."

"Well, I – I mean we – might be," Justin said. "Look through the windows in the door. I figured out how to get the doors open without the motor, but as soon as I roll it up, those freaks will start rolling in."

There were now about twenty zombies all together. The beginning of them were passing the first of the four bay doors and staggering towards Jerry and the truck.

"Screw it," Isherwood said, losing his patience. "Open up the last door. We'll beat 'em to punch."

"Aye, aye, Cap'n," Justin said, immediately jumping up and catching hold of a thick chain. As he dropped back to the floor, the twenty foot metal door had risen about three feet. They couldn't tell if Jerry had noticed the door opening or not. Justin kept at it. Isherwood rolled out from under the door with his axe, just as it was opening another few feet.

Behind him, Isherwood could hear the truck's engine noise increase slightly, as well as the clanking of the gate rising. They should be almost home free, but he was going to be their insurance policy. Unlike before, he didn't wait for the first zombie to drift into his strike zone. He came out swinging. The first skull dislodged cleanly from the shoulders of an older white man in overalls. Instead of arresting his momentum and re-swinging, he finished his rotation three hundred sixty degrees into the head of his next target, like a whirling dervish.

He sheared off the cap of a large black woman's skull and decapitated a skinny high schooler with his next swings. There was a gap between him and the next wave.

"Isherwood, come on!" Patrick called to him. Isherwood looked back to see the rear of the truck disappearing into the dim light of the bay as the door rolled shut behind it. "Slide on into home."

He grabbed the handle of his axe with both hands and ran towards the bay door, which was again only about three feet from the ground. He tucked one leg behind him and slid under the door, or at least mostly under. The concrete was rough and slowed his slide, but Patrick pulled him in the rest of the way, just as Justin slammed the door down the last few feet.

"Phew!" Justin smiled, clapping his torn up hands. "That was a tight little maneuver, but we *did it*. Who's ready to go shopping?"

"Y'all go on ahead. If you won't be needing my help with the blow torch, think I'll just take myself a siesta in the truck," Jerry said from the driver's door.

"Sounds good, Uncle," Isherwood said. "We'll come getcha if the security grill separating us from the rest of the store gives us any issues."

As the driver's door slammed closed behind them, the younger men hurried back through the door to the check-out counter. Justin, for his part, slid across the counter.

"Come and get it!" Justin yelled into the huge cavern of the rest of the store. He shook the security gate as he did it. "Ring-a-ding-ding. Dinner! One chubby white boy with a side of ginger. Cooome and get it."

"Am I the side of ginger?" Patrick asked.

"Aren't you red-headed?" Justin asked.

"Uh, no."

"Really? No way. All this time. But your beard's red, right?"

"No, not really."

"Shoot, well. Your name's Patrick, ain't it? You must be Irish."

"Okay, whatever."

"Hey, guys. Not to interrupt," Isherwood spoke up. "But, uh. I'm starting to think the controls for that door are on the other side of it."

"Really?" Justin asked. "Let me take a look." He slapped the security grill a couple more times for good measure. He took a couple steps backward sizing up the gate. "Nah, look – the chain hoist is on this side, but dang. It's really high up there. Isherwood, you've got long arms. Can you reach?"

"Fat chance," Isherwood scoffed.

"Stop calling me fat," Justin pushed his eyebrows upward and popped out his lower lip.

"I wasn't! I didn't mean – aahhh!" Isherwood grimaced. "Every. Stinking. Time."

"No, but really," Justin said, quickly changing tact. "There's just this padlock, and then we can pull it up. There's some hooks or something in the floor, but those just wiggle out. It's all yours, axe-man."

"Man," Isherwood said. "This is gonna notch the heck out of this nice, new axe. But," he hesitated. His face suddenly brightened. "But, I'll soon have my pick of replacements." At the last word, he let the axe fly without even a practice swing. It missed the mark by several inches, so he tried again squaring his feet perpendicular to the gate. He took a practice swing. And then another swing. And another. Sparks kept flying, but the padlock was holding.

"Trouble in paradise?" Justin asked.

"Yup," Isherwood said, lowering the axe to the floor and catching his breath. "This isn't working."

"Hey, guys," Patrick called out. "Before you get too far along raising this thing, we got company." Black figures were beginning to emerge from the shadows and rake their rotting fingertips against the far side of the security grill. "Gross," Patrick continued. "They're drooling all over the place. If I slip in this crap..." he trailed off, mumbling to himself about eye juices.

"Look here," Justin said. "I've got an idea. Might've seen this on *Die Hard Five* or *Six*, I can't remember. Or maybe it was *Kindergarten Cop*? Who knows. Let me see that axe and your mini-sledge."

Patrick handed over the sledgehammer, leaving his friends at the gate to rummage among the spare tools in the maintenance bays. "I'm gonna get myself a sweet hunting knife out of that cabinet in sporting goods," he was saying to himself. "Always loved looking at all those knives as a kid, but never had much money or use for a second pocket knife, let alone one of those nice, long Bowie knives. Oh yeah, gonna get a hip holster for it, too. But," he said, grabbing a long tool out of the drawers of a red steel mechanic's tool chest. "*This* will do nicely until I get one."

Patrick walked calmly back to the security grill carrying a 28-inch Phillips head screwdriver. "Guys, look. This is like the perfect tool for this. Watch."

Justin turned away from his efforts at unsuccessfully stuffing the handle of the axe into the shackle of the padlock. As he and Isherwood watched, Patrick rammed the screwdriver into the eye socket of one of the Wal-Mart zombies.

"That's probably the longest screwdriver I've ever—" Isherwood began.

"*Shhh!*" Patrick raised a finger. "Watch this part."

The zombie fell backwards as the metal shaft of the screwdriver hit home, but as it fell, Patrick let go, and the zombie's head slid off the screwdriver as the grip caught between the horizontal metal rods of the security grill. The screwdriver was just resting on the grill, waiting for its next target. "Awesome, right?" Patrick smiled, admiring his handiwork.

Isherwood nodded, too, in admiration.

"Gnarly," Justin added.

"I know, right?" Patrick said, thrusting the screwdriver into another Walmartian skull.

"This isn't gonna work," Justin said. "But all I need is a piece of metal that tapers to a point, and I'm home free."

"Go look through the drawers of the tool boxes," Patrick advised. "There're like a million different tools in the shop."

Justin came back a couple seconds later with a handful of tools. "You were right, dude. This place is loaded. This file should work."

"I'm almost done here, guys," Patrick said. "Do your worst."

Justin shoved the point of the file down into the shackle of the padlock. "Wanna hold this for me?" He smiled, winking at Isherwood. He then took the sledge hammer and pounded down on the wider end of the file. After three or so knocks, the padlock clattered open.

"Nice," Isherwood said. "Didn't even need my umbrella."

They waited a while longer rattling the bars of the grill until the trickle of oncoming zombies finally stopped. "Alright, fat kids," Justin said, "Welcome to the candy store!"

They rolled up the grill and shoved the bodies to the side, so they could lower the grill back in place. They decided to stack up the bodies later. Isherwood sprinted off to the gun cases in the sporting goods department, and Patrick followed after him. Patrick still arrived several strides ahead of Isherwood. Justin, for his part, walked and stood in the middle of one of the five main side aisles, letting the moment soak in. He, too, definitely felt the itch to help raid the firearms and ammunition, but there was something else, too.

Isherwood also took a moment of his own to behold the glory of the gun displays. Patrick, for his part, took the sledge hammer to the knife display upon arrival.

"I can't believe it, Patty O'Hooligan. It's untouched. Completely, actually untouched. *All* at our fingertips. Ohhh, man." Isherwood whacked the latches and padlocks off all the plexi-glass doors and sliding cabinets. He paused for a second, thinking. "Dangit. One sec – I need just one more thing to make this perfect."

Isherwood made to run off but stopped.

"Looking for some of these?" Justin smiled, as he rolled five or six nested shopping carts down the aisle.

"Yes! Justin, you magnificent man, you read my mind. How can we have a shopping spree without *shopping* carts? Now, it's perfect." He hurried back over to one of the glass cabinets. "First, a stocking stuffer: one awesome set of binoculars."

"Here," Patrick said, handing a hunting knife and sheath to each of them. "Loop these into your belts, just in case we get any more surprise visitors."

There were two rotating displays of guns, and Isherwood and Justin were each at one of them, slowly turning the rotating gun racks, mesmerized. "No ARs, of course," Justin observed. "It's Wal-Mart after all, but dang. Just dang."

Isherwood picked up another .308 Winchester with scope like Monsignor's, but newer, and placed it in his basket. Next, he added a .30-06 Springfield with a hard rubber stock and scope, bolt-action. He picked up a 270 next. It didn't have a scope, but it was camouflaged. Isherwood really wanted to raid the pistols next, but needed to get Sara's bow next. Then he noticed, frowning, that Wal-Mart didn't sell handguns.

He took an empty basket with him to the fishing aisle and filled it with every bowfishing product imaginable, including the store's entire stock of broadheads and arrows. He ran the cart over to the automotive section, and hurried back to the guns. This time, he starting tapping all the padlocks off the ammunition cases. At first, he was careful. But soon, he was dropping armloads into the basket. He quickly regressed, though, when he saw the mess he was making.

"Alright, guys," Patrick said and had to repeat himself. When Isherwood and Justin finally pulled themselves away from the gun displays and ammo cases, they noticed that Patrick's entire belt was full of knives.

"Where're you headed, Dundee?" Justin asked him.

"I'm gonna grab every big plastic container I can and fill them with salt, curing salt, sea salt – basically all the salt in the store – plus vinegar and water. Then, I'm gonna dump in whatever meat still looks salvageable. Oh, and I'll probably use the knives, too."

"Wow, that's genius," Isherwood said. "How'd you know to do all that?"

"Well, your Gran and I were talking about it after our trip to Langlois yesterday, plus there's a set of encyclopedias in Monsignor's study. I just scaled it up a bit. Actually, you know, it was the bard that inspired me:

'She hath eaten up all her beef, and she is herself in the tub.' *Measure for Measure*."

"Whoa." Isherwood was shaking his head. "That's all — wow. I'm super impressed. We'll do that at Langlois, too, then."

"What's a bard?" Justin asked, looking through a scope up at one of the sky lights.

Patrick didn't answer him, but started mumbling something about a "tub of infamy."

CHAPTER TWELVE:
NEW GREEN

Jerry, it had turned out, wasn't able to take the nap he had wanted in the truck while the boys went on their shopping spree. Instead, he had spent his time making some modifications to Justin's blue Chevy, or what used to be a blue Chevy. He had grabbed an armful of black matte finish spray paint cans from the Paint department, spurning the rolls of blue painter's tape that were also within easy reach. After giving the truck a new coat of paint, concealing the bright blue and the chrome accents, he located a full set of replacement tires. Finding a battery-operated drill that still held a charge, he installed mounting brackets all around the sides of the truck. He hung four spare tires and wheels on each side of the truck, two whole sets. Next, he tore apart and disassembled a chain link enclosure and metal pole that stood at the corner of the automotive department. It had probably been used at some point to store returned items or unruly customers, but was now empty. He sprayed all that down with the black spray paint, as well, and mounted it along the inside of the bed of the truck. Jerry was able to screw in or bolt most of the fencing onto the truck, but he secured the rest with his welding supplies. He added a couple more mounting brackets to the top of the cab to snap an aluminum ladder onto. He was just putting the finishing touches on a grill guard when the creaking wheels of shopping carts signaled the return of the shoppers.

"Whoa," Isherwood said, leaning against the door frame in amazement. The sun had moved past noon, and the light from the skylights was starting to fade, but they could still see the truck clear enough.

"What's that?" Justin said in confusion. "Where'd my truck go?"

"*That* is your truck," Isherwood explained. Justin only needed momentary consoling, as he began to wrap his mind about the magnitude of the job Jerry had done.

Jerry eventually noticed them and pulled up his welding hood. "Couldn't fall asleep," he explained, standing back to admire his handiwork. "It's no Old Red, but it'll do."

"It needs a name," Patrick decided aloud, as he began loading up the bed of the truck with all their new acquisitions. "Man, we've got a lot more storage room now. I'm gonna run back and grab every box of cereal and bag of rice I can. We can just throw it atop all our new gear since we've got this metal cage now."

"How about the zombie-mobile or the Mystery Machine?" Isherwood offered lamely.

"Let Justin name it," Jerry said, as he went about picking up his tools.

"How about Old Blue?" Justin said, bowing his head in reverence.

Isherwood raised an eyebrow. "It's really not blue at all anymore, though, is it?"

Justin shook his head. "*That's* why it's 'OLD Blue.' Sheesh."

"Whatever, man," Isherwood clapped him on the shoulder. "Let's load up. We may still have time to make a pass by the car dealership."

Jerry perked up. "The tractor dealership?"

Isherwood grimaced, thinking about it. The John Deere dealership was at the other end of Hospital Road. He didn't want to risk driving up Hospital Road in broad daylight, but they could probably take the back way. They could go north up Major Parkway as they had the other day, but instead of turning right for the bridge, go left towards the Morganza Highway. That would also take them by a couple gas stations.

"Okay. Let's grab some extra fuel cans while we're here in the Automotive Department. We'll make a gas run, and use the opportunity to check out the zed situation around the end of Hospital Road."

"Grab a hand pump, too," Jerry added. "That should work on those underground tanks. Gasoline will be crap soon. Diesel lasts a hell of a lot longer. Less volatile."

"The airport's out that way, too," Patrick added, returning with his first cart of cereal boxes. "We'll need to check that out eventually."

Isherwood's head was starting to swim with ideas and things that still needed doing. He hadn't even thought about the airport yet. He doubted the planes still left in the hangars would be much good for anything without adhering to a regular maintenance schedule. Hadn't his Grandad and Uncle Jimmy always talked about that? Both were pilots. Jimmy was pretty close in age to Isherwood despite being his uncle. He was a helicopter pilot for the Louisiana National Guard, actually he was the battalion commander for the state's whole fleet of assault and rescue helicopters. When everything started going down, they knew Jimmy would be in the thick of it, for better or worse, and they hadn't heard from his family since. Isherwood knew that if Jimmy were still alive, he'd be trying to get to Gran, his mother, as soon as humanly possible. Gran and Lizzy had left a note on the kitchen counter telling whoever might come by that they'd moved to St. Mary's. But it had been a long time since they'd heard helicopter blades overhead.

A thought like a stroke of thunder just reverberated through Isherwood's mind. "Oh my God!" He said aloud to no one in particular. "The National Guard outpost. I forgot all about it. We've got to go there next. Screw the car dealership. They've got armored vehicles, transports, *and* —"

"An armory," Justin said, his eyes lighting up.

*****

98

It turned out that there was more zombie activity at the end of Hospital Road than they had hoped to encounter. Jerry was helping Isherwood locate the underground tanks and figure out how to use the hand pump. Justin and Patrick circled around them taking out the two or three zombies that were coming every five minutes or so. Patrick was testing out the dozen or so knives he had slipped onto his belt. Justin was sighting in the scope of a Savage Mark II .22 rifle he had taken from Wal-Mart, using exploding zombie heads to test his accuracy.

After about half an hour, they were able to fill the tank of the truck, which was still at half a tank, with the hand pump. After filling one of the spare fuel tanks almost halfway, Justin called over to Isherwood that the zombie action was getting a little too hot. Instead of twos and threes, the zombies were beginning to come, mostly from the direction of Hospital Road, in groups of five or more.

They packed up quickly and stowed their gear in Old Blue. Before they left, Isherwood grabbed one of the cans of black spray paint that Jerry had been using to paint the truck. He ran over to the entrance of the gas station where there was a broad expanse of concrete. He began by drawing a long line roughly pointed in the direction of St. Mary's. He added a loop to the line making it a giant 'P' and then added another two lines. These formed an 'X' which intersected with the 'P'. It was a giant Chi-Rho.

Justin was slowly backing away from a growing crowd of zombies. "That's enough doodling, Isherwood."

*****

Jerry was insistent that, since they were within spitting distance of the John Deere dealership, that they find a way to pass by it. Isherwood resisted as daylight was growing short, but eventually relented. He led them onto the Morganza Highway heading west. They laid on the horn, trying to get as many of the zombies to follow them as possible. Next, they turned up Airport Road with a fair crop of followers. This gave Patrick the chance he had wanted to survey the airstrip, hangars, and support buildings of the rural airport. They were going slowly again, less than ten miles per hour, so the horde could keep up with them.

When Airport Road ended at the River Road – the same road wound around past the bridge and on all the way to New Orleans – they turned south onto the River Road. After another half mile or so, they gunned it, making the loop back to the Morganza Highway and Hospital Road. They crossed over a set of railroad tracks which marked the northern end of Hospital Road. The John Deere dealership was just on the other side of the tracks.

They turned into a u-shaped driveway of the John Deere place. It was nearing 4pm. The driveway marked the edges of a man-made hill on which several models of tractors were displayed.

"The one out front would do just fine," Jerry said, as they rummaged through the front office. "It's got the right tilling implement already latched on. It's probably got some fuel in it already, too."

Isherwood was starting to understand. Uncle Jerry had passed by those display models probably a hundred thousand times in his life. He had seen other farmers, bigger and more successful farmers, buying tractors right off the showroom floor. All the while, buying a brand new tractor had been unthinkable. He had been fighting with the same old tractor for decades. That bright green John Deere paint had been teasing this man, Isherwood thought, his whole life. But not anymore.

"Got it," Isherwood called out, pulling a set of keys out of a desk drawer. "The tag says DISPLAY."

The young men fanned out around the small hill as Jerry climbed the hill and into the cab of a large green tractor. It seemed more like a tank than a tractor, Isherwood thought. Instead of tires, the tractor had four sets of tracks. It seemed a little big for the church grounds. He didn't know if Jerry planned on plowing fields or zombies.

Jerry locked himself in the Command View cab, and turned the key in the ignition. Amazingly, the tractor roared to life. He drove the tractor clear off the hill and onto Hospital Road. The tractor was disappearing over the railroad tracks before the rest of them realized what was happening.

"Alright, guys. We better follow him, because I don't think he plans on stopping."

"He, uh –? Hey, what about the –?" Patrick stammered. "He gave us back the keys to Old Blue, right?"

CHAPTER THIRTEEN: INDEFECTABILITY

"I'm really enjoying our coffee dates, Smithy," Sara said pretending to be bashful. She and Isherwood were strolling through the Prayer Garden.

The garden was situated nearly at the center of the church grounds. The rectory, the church office, and the parish hall formed sort of an 'L' shape and the prayer garden was tucked into the corner of the 'L'. It was the spot where they had helped hide Easter eggs for the kids. A tall cross stood on a brick plinth at the center of the garden. The cross rose from the center of a rectangular green lawn, which was surrounded by rings of azaleas and crape myrtles. A grove of tall pine trees led away from the garden into open fields.

The garden had often served as a backdrop to their relationship. It was full of stone and cast iron benches, which Sara thought were very romantic. They had had a couple dates here. They had even taken some of their engagement pictures there. Even now that it had become their backyard, it seemed like it had always been so.

Isherwood was smiling and nodding. "Yeah, it really helps me clear my mind for the day. Helps me think straight."

"What *are* you thinking about doing today?" She asked, as Uncle Jerry's tractor hummed in the fields somewhere beyond the garden.

"Might just help with the planting. Maybe raid Tractor Supply for seed potatoes and seed packets. Hey, what if we needed to chop down some of the pine trees around the garden?"

"Why would you do that?"

"For more sunlight on the fields."

Sara was shaking her head. "I'd say no, but I don't think I'll need to," she said mysteriously. Isherwood chuckled and nodded in resignation. He knew better than to prod the momma bear.

After a moment, he asked, "So?"

"*So* what?"

"*Sooo?*" Isherwood asked again.

Comprehension suddenly warmed across Sara's face. Her whole face broke into a smile, and she pulled Isherwood's arm in for a tighter embrace. "You mean my bowhunting gear? You remembered! That was so thoughtful of you – three hundred pounds of thoughtful. You took everything they had, didn't you?"

Isherwood was basking in the warmth of his wife's appreciation. He was nodding with pride and smiling stupidly. "Oh yeah. Like the Grinch who stole the last can of Who-hash."

Sara took a moment to go over all the different pieces of equipment that had first caught her eye. Then, shaking her head as if remembering something important, she looked down at her watch. "Uh-oh! Come on," she said, tugging Isherwood behind her. "We'll be *late* for morning prayer!"

"Morning *what?*"

*****

Monsignor had tapped Isherwood on the shoulder after morning prayer. They were talking together in the sacristy, a small room adjacent to the altar of the church, where the priest's robes were stored, as well as the gold dishes for Mass. Monsignor was nodding, as he prepared the dishes for Mass. "That's right, Isherwood. I'll be continuing to celebrate Mass every day at noon – priests are really supposed to say or go to Mass every day. But I've added morning and evening prayer, as well – actually, I'm going easy on everybody. It's technically mid-morning prayer, "Terce," and Vespers at 6pm, either before or after dinner depending on when you all can finishing wiping off the guts and gore."

Isherwood laughed at that. "I'm not sure one ever finishes cleaning off some things. Just ask Patrick about the eye juice."

Monsignor fell quiet as he walked glass pitchers of wine and water up a couple steps to the altar. "Oh, let me help you with that," Isherwood said, taking the pitchers to the side table beside the altar. "I suppose I'll be helping as an altar boy, anyway. But Monsignor, I was thinking about it just now during prayer. I really think you're on to something. We really need things like this to bring our community together, and to order and structure the day – even the year, as the liturgical calendar goes. Otherwise, why keep a seven-day week, or a twelve month calendar, or any of it?"

"You thought through all that just during morning prayer?" Monsignor asked in his way.

Isherwood had to laugh, knowing that the old priest always perceived much more than he let on. "No, you're right. I've been thinking a lot about how we go forward. Who 'we' is and will be."

"I'm sure it's already occurred to you, Isherwood, that this is not the first time mankind has faced a plague or even a cataclysmic event."

Isherwood was quiet for a long time mulling over Monsignor's words. "Monsignor, you know – I was wondering about apostolic succession during all this, this stuff. Apostles elected new apostles, the bishops elected new bishops, the pope began appointing new bishops – an unbroken chain back to the beginning, but what happens now? If the pope is gone and the cardinals are gone, too, without anybody to elect a new pope, if all or mostly all of the bishops are gone, who names new bishops? Are you the de facto bishop now?"

"An interesting question, given the state of things. I think I know somebody who could figure out the answer to that question."

Isherwood opened his eyes wide in surprise. "Really? Another survivor? A priest? You've heard from him somehow? *Who is it?*"

Monsignor was chuckling to himself. "It's *you*, Isherwood."

Isherwood dropped his head to his chest in mock exasperation, and Monsignor threw his head backward in laughter. Isherwood tried to resist, but couldn't help joining in.

"You will let me know if I'm a bishop, won't you?" Monsignor kept laughing.

"You'll need a change of headgear, for sure."

"And a staff."

"I know a guy with a pretty fierce frog-gigging pole."

CHAPTER FOURTEEN: COUNTDOWN

I sherwood's mind was humming with what Monsignor had said for the rest of the day. He had some more things he wanted to talk over with Monsignor, but they would have to wait. He forcibly cleared his mind.

The "Three Amigos," as Justin had taken to calling them over everyone's objections, were tasked with exploring the eastern end of Main Street. Tadd had taken Isherwood aside for a very one-directional discussion. Thereafter, it appeared Jerry would be staying within the church grounds for the time being. This was just as good, Isherwood thought, as he knew Jerry would be busy tilling the ground from safe inside the cab of his new tractor.

The plan for the Three Amigos was to call out for any survivors that might still be hiding along the road between Langlois' grocery and the township of Waterloo. They had taken a map of the parish and divided it into a search grid. They would take one section per day, calling out for survivors. They would also catalogue possible honey pots of supplies and undertake a general survey of the area.

Before they could start down the road east, however, there were two places on their list to visit: the car dealership and the National Guard armory. Justin had also mentioned the sheriff's and police stations would likely have armories, too, but these would have to wait.

"Let's just all go inside," Patrick said, as Isherwood succeeded in prying open the glass door of the Maggio Oldsmobile showroom. "If the zombies get thick on this side, we'll just tap on the glass and guide them to the other side."

"You know, my family used to own this dealership. My great-grandfather, Bert Loriot, started it. Loriot Chevrolet, it was called. If you don't mind, I'd like to take a second to reclaim it." Justin and Patrick looked down in surprise at Isherwood's left hand. He had taken out a can of black spray paint from somewhere inside his sack and was shaking it, rattling the ball inside ferociously.

Justin tilted his hands back in a sign of indifference. "That's cool, man. But you better make me a cherry deal on a new Caddie, or I'm walking."

"Gonna rename the town, too?" Patrick asked, tapping his elbow into Justin's side as they laughed quietly at Isherwood behind his back. Isherwood was spray painting in large, eight-foot letters across the solid wall of windows that marked the front of the dealership.

"Actually, funny you should mention it," Isherwood laughed as he swept out the cross bar of the 'T' in Smith, and soon to be the 'T' in "Smith Chevrolet." "But I've been thinking about that."

"Of course he has," Justin said shaking his head. "This guy."

"Let's do it," Patrick said dramatically. "We'll break in to City Hall – I mean, it's only a block from the church. We'll do it in the City Council chambers. We'll elect a new mayor and council members, also granting to each councilman plenary powers and ownership over their precinct. We'll change the town charter. No big."

Isherwood rocked his head back and forth in semi-agreement. "That could work. Not sure about plenary powers and ownership, though. We'll probably be living communally for the foreseeable future."

"Socialism. Always socialism," Justin announced with mock fury.

107

"More like a monastery," Isherwood winked back at them. Noticing something in his voice, Justin and Patrick just looked at each other in quiet confusion.

"Well," Justin said, shaking it off. He turned around to behold the glittering edifice that stood at the center of the showroom. A fully loaded Cadillac Escalade. A thin skin of dust was coating the $80,000 vehicle.

"Age cannot wither her, nor custom stale," Patrick said, following Justin.

"It is the east, and my Caddie the sun," Justin remarked as he popped open the door, and filled his lungs with a deep breath of the new car smell.

"Hey!" Patrick frowned. "Yesterday, you asked what a bard was and today you're quoting Shakespeare?"

"That's right! And don't call me Shirley." Justin was reaching to other side of the steering column. "I wonder," he said, "could we be so luck—?" He was interrupted by the twinkling sound of keys waiting for him in the ignition. Justin hopped in the vehicle, giddy as a schoolboy. He turned the keys in the ignition and listened to the engine roar to life with an ethereal look on his face.

"Dibs," he said.

*****

Patrick passed on picking out a new vehicle, opting instead to take Justin's Old Blue. Justin barely noticed the passing of Old Blue from his possession, as he was clearly having some sort of religious experience inside his new vehicle.

Isherwood knew exactly what he wanted – had always wanted since watching MacGyver as a kid. A Jeep Wrangler. There was only one Jeep among the dealership's used car inventory, judging from the rows of keys hanging inside the general manager's office. It just happened to be exactly what Isherwood wanted for the Apocalypse. He stood holding the laminated yellow key tag as if it were a Wonka Golden Ticket. The tag read "Jeep Wrangler Ext." It wasn't exactly what "Mac" drove, Isherwood explained, but they needed the extra space.

They realized that, even if they found armored vehicles at the National Guard Armory, they were each already driving a vehicle. They decided to hold off on the armory until the next day, and push east along Main Street. Besides, to frustrate thieves, the dealership kept less than an eighth a tank of gasoline in each of the vehicles. They would need to stop at the LA Express station along the way.

Patrick took point, and Justin in his new Escalade and Isherwood in his jeep followed behind him. They followed New Roads Street down past the dealership and around the corner where Regions Bank stood. They turned back on to Main Street and it was a short trip, less than a mile, to the gas station.

Thanks to Jerry's modifications, Old Blue had become exceedingly efficient at mowing down the zombies. Isherwood observed the remnants of zombies left in the truck's wake. Skulls weren't always crushed in the process, but every zombie that encountered Old Blue was permanently slowed down. Problem was, Isherwood mused, these zombies would become a menace. They were the kind that would drag themselves off somewhere to rot. Later, when searching a backyard, they would suddenly emerge from underneath a bush or raised house, disturbing a little pile of dog and cat bones, and bite through a foot or calf.

There were fewer zombies the farther they went along Main Street. Only two or three could be seen hobbling about in the vicinity of the LA Express. Patrick parked Old Blue in the middle of the street. He slid out of Old Blue and jumped into the bed where he would have a full 360 degree view of the area. He took one of the .22 rifles from the gun rack hanging against the back window. "A little target practice," he whispered to himself.

Isherwood and Justin pulled into the center of the LA Express parking lot, facing opposite directions around what looked like the cover to the underground gas tank. Isherwood opened up the back of the jeep and pulled out the hand pump they had picked up at Wal-Mart.

Isherwood fed one of the eight-foot black rubber hoses down into the tank. Justin took the other one and fed it into his gas tank. Isherwood began turning the crank. It wasn't turning as quickly or as quietly as it had the other day.

"Ten turns per gallon, eh?" Justin asked. "Look. I'm gonna run into the store and get you some WD-40."

"I need your help, Justin. Wouldn't mind somebody watching my back, too."

"It's okay, man. You've got Patrick in the crow's nest over there."

"He can't see *between* the vehicles, though."

"I'll be *right* back," Justin said, grabbing a crow bar and disappearing around the jeep.

Isherwood rolled his eyes. "Thanks, buddy."

Isherwood listened and waited to the strange orchestra of Patrick's periodic firing and the rhythmic cranking of the pump. He was counting to two hundred, maybe two hundred fifty, estimating the Escalade's fuel tank to be somewhere between twenty and twenty-five gallons.

At about 90, Justin popped the lock open on the metal frame glass door. Around 120, a hunk of re-animated flesh fell from the underside of the Cadillac. By 140, the bloody torso, arm stump, and head had become aware of Isherwood, and began dragging itself towards the cranking. At 160, the thing had emerged from under the vehicle. At 165, Justin located the WD-40 and immediately began thinking to himself how good a Snickers bar would taste. At 180, the half zombie was a foot behind Isherwood and swung a bloody stump towards him. The bone protruding from the end of the stump was just millimeters from grazing Isherwood's back. At 200, Justin thought to himself, *Screw it, I want a Coke, too.* At 215, a splash of gas spurted out the Escalade's gas tank.

Isherwood stood up to remove the hose from the tank, and shook violently as he first noticed the thing that had crept up behind him and the long blood streak trailing away from it. He dropped the hose and gasoline began dribbling out of the end. He pulled out his 9mm from its holster and aimed. At what would have been 225 turns of the crank,

Justin had reached Isherwood with a Snickers bar still hanging out of his mouth.

Justin grabbed Isherwood's arm. *"Donnadoitstopputcannitseealluvagas."* He mumbled from a full mouth. He pushed Isherwood behind him, grabbed a knife from his belt, and shoved it into the thing's skull.

"Whoa. What gives?" Even as Isherwood said it, he realized that the gas had spilled near enough the half zombie that even a small spark could have sent a column of flame streaking down to the tank beneath them.

Justin swallowed hard. "You almost just launched us to the moon. I can't leave you anywhere."

"That's exactly —" Isherwood grumbled in frustration. He stopped short as he noticed the extra Snickers bars hanging out of Justin's jeans pocket. "Hey, give me one of those. I need something to do while I watch you fill up my gas tank."

CHAPTER FIFTEEN:
UNION

"You know," Isherwood said, as Justin finished filling the jeep and the rest of the spare gas tanks. "If we just went to Wickcliffe, the country club, and back looking for survivors, we might still have enough daylight left to check out the armory."

"What?" Justin asked, smiling as he placed the full fuel tanks in the back of the jeep. "Your little brush with death, making you rethink your life?"

"A little bit, yeah. Did you lock the store back up?" Justin looked suddenly suspicious and went back to the door to seal it up. As he did, Isherwood whistled over to Patrick to let him know they were saddling up the horses. Patrick gave a thumbs-up and racked the rifle.

After another mile or so they crossed Patin Dyke, which under normal conditions helped regulate the water level of False River. They stopped briefly here to survey the operation, as well as the intersection of Main Street and the road that led to Ventress and Jarreau, the two smallish towns on the far side of False River. The long lake, for all intents and purposes, ended near the dyke and fed into two small bayous, which continued the lake's outline into the Mississippi River levee. The same thing happened on the other side of the lake as well.

Half an hour later, they were passing back through the same spot. Surprisingly, however, they had picked up another passenger on their way back. It was a young black boy, maybe seven or eight years old. Patrick had to swerve hard to prevent hitting him, as he ran right into the road as though something was pursuing him. And probably was. His eyes opened wide as he realized a pack of white guys were his savior. He looked like he might even turn back toward whatever he'd been running from, but Justin scooped him up and put him in the passenger seat of the Escalade. The boy had yet to say anything to any of them.

*****

"Don't forget the flashlights," Isherwood advised, as they climbed out of their vehicles at the National Guard Armory. They had parked a half block away from the armory. The number of zombies was visibly thicker here, Patrick had noticed still driving the lead vehicle.

"Hey, little buddy," Justin asked the little black boy they had found on the way back into St. Maryville. "You gonna come with us? Or stay here?" The little boy suddenly shifted in his seat at the sound of gunfire. It was Patrick beginning to clear the area from the bed of Old Blue. The truck was parked facing the armory, so the roof of the cab provided an excellent rifle rest.

The little boy shifted again. This time he slid from the seat to the carpeted floor. He tucked himself so far under the dashboard that Justin could only see the boy's scared eyes peering out at him. "Okay, little bro. Stay there and stay quiet, and you should be fine. I'd leave you with a pistol, but that seems like a bad idea, somehow. Take this knife, though. Okay?"

The little boy shook his head. "Come on, little man. Just in case, okay? It won't bite you."

The little boy shook his head again. Justin couldn't tell what the boy was doing, until something shined out of the darkness. The boy was showing him he already had a knife – a big one, too.

"Alrighty, then," Justin nodded to himself, as he closed the door of the Escalade behind him. "Maybe I won't be letting you play with my kids, after all." He mumbled to himself.

"Looks like the doors to the place are wide open," Patrick said looking through the scope of the rifle.

Isherwood sighed. "That's probably a bad sign. I think this place probably ended up serving as an emergency shelter, once General Hospital devolved into a bloodbath. They probably started triaging the bitten, and we know what happens after that."

"The place is slowly emptying in this direction," Patrick told them after squeezing off another couple of rounds. "You could probably loop around the back and enter without being seen."

"You sure we even want to go in there?" Justin asked. "It's probably a house of horrors. I think I can hear the flies buzzing from here."

Isherwood shook his head in indecision. "Let's help Patrick ring the dinner bell a bit first. The zed crowd looks like it's starting to thicken. But we have to get to that armory before someone else can. There will probably be some automatic rifles scattered among the dead that we'll need to gather up, too."

"You got it, dude," Justin relented. He hopped into the bed of the truck and pulled another .22 from the gun rack.

After another couple of rounds, Patrick was reloading. "All this time, you haven't reloaded yet?" Isherwood said from the tailgate, where he was cleaning up the dead straggling up the road behind them.

Over the next half hour or so, each of them was forced to reload at least once. "That place just never seems to empty. It's not like the doors were locked or even closed. Why would they not have scattered over time?"

"Something's rotten in Denmark. Clearly," Patrick replied. Then, realizing what he had done, "I'm sorry, guys – there's like a Shakespeare quote for everything."

There was soon an extended pause in the flow of zombies coming from in and around the armory. They left the trucks behind, as well as the little boy. Justin looked back to see his eyes peeking out just above the dashboard. They immediately disappeared again.

They found the first uniformed guardsmen near the front door. "At least they didn't turn," Patrick said at the grisly sight.

"They never had a chance." Isherwood frowned, looking down at the odd collection of still-uniformed body parts. "They were probably swarmed, poor guys. True to their posts until the end. At some point, we're gonna have to honor the dead with proper burials."

"I was wondering when you'd get to that part," Justin said with feigned exhaustion in his voice. "Gross, you could at least leave what's left of them alone."

"I told you I was going to collect up the firearms. It doesn't bother you when people in the movies leave guns behind all the time?"

"Gahh! I *hate* that," Patrick said, bending down to help out.

"Well, sure. I just think we have plenty enough already."

Isherwood stood back up, checking out the condition of the pistol and automatic rifle he had retrieved. "Maybe for now, but we've gotta think long term."

"Figures," Patrick said, fingering a pistol he had found. "Magazine's empty. They must've fought to the bitter end."

"*Shhh!* Wait," Justin said from just inside the door. There was a short hallway before another set of glass doors opening into a wide assembly hall. Justin had turned on his flashlight and was shining it into the darkness of the hall. They followed him in, finding another pair of firearms as they went.

"I think I can hear what was drawing them in or *keeping* them in. There's something rattling around in there."

"By all means let's go into the dark following a funny noise," Patrick said with actual enthusiasm.

They stood still together in a line as their eyes slowly adjusted to the dim light. Justin's flashlight was slowly scanning the large, gymnasium-like hall. There were lines of narrow windows along either side of the walls, but only a little light was coming through. It was overcast. Justin had been right about the flies, as well. As their eyes adjusted, they began to comprehend the carnage around them. There were lines of flipped cots and a maelstrom of supplies and rations, but the single most common thing littering the floor was rotting meat. Even now, the floor was sticky with blood.

Isherwood choked. "It's like a scene from a Kubrick movie."

"Yeah," Patrick agreed. "Like that elevator of blood in *The Shining*. Tidal wave splashing up the walls. The smell, though – the movie couldn't tell us about that. Shows us just how accustomed we've become to all this crap."

Justin shook his head. "A few years of fatherhood were enough to stall my gag reflex. I'd almost rather this than a nursery full of kids exploding with a stomach bug." The rest of them nodded in agreement. Their eyes fluttered with memories. "Y'all ready? I think the noise – whatever it is – is coming from inside one of those metal cages. It might just be an alarm clock."

"I can't believe how easy it is to herd those things up." Isherwood raised his hand in disgust. "A stupid alarm clock? Are you serious? If the human race had known about this weakness, we could've survived."

"Hey," Patrick said. "I resent that. *We* did survive. I'm still here, aren't I?"

"The son of man," Isherwood smiled distractedly, as he began searching through the junk left behind for guns and ammo. He had turned his flashlight on. "You know," he said. "I might just pass on all this mess. Go straight for the armory." He headed back to the entrance and began arranging the useful supplies he had found on one of the few clear spots on the ground. Coming back in the gymnasium hall, he found Patrick and Justin staring into one of the metal cages against the wall. The cages, like individual prison cells, probably once served as materiel storage lockers but were now mostly empty.

"Looks like he survived in here for a week or more," Justin was saying. "Dude, fought off starvation probably on MREs before finally putting a bullet in his head. Can you imagine being shut up in that little

116

cage, surrounded by these things all this time?" They had followed the tiny sound of the alarm to a storage locker, where a black uniformed man lay curled up on the ground around a radio backpack. The radio was emitting a constant hum of static – it was the noise they had been hearing.

"Bullet?" Patrick asked. "I don't see any wounds."

"Dude," Isherwood said sternly, pushing his way between them. "He's still breathing."

"He's *what?*" Justin said looking back down in surprise. "Are you kidding me? Let's get him out of there. Probably needs water. If he's lasted this long, God knows what he's been drinking."

"That's weird," Patrick said, tugging at the lock that had been holding the door latch in place. "It's padlocked from the outside."

"Either he's a criminal, then, or somebody stuffed him in there to protect him," Isherwood thought aloud.

Patrick ran off saying he was going to grab the triangular file and the mini-sledge. A couple seconds later, Justin and Isherwood heard shots being fired and ran off after him. Patrick appeared to be in no serious danger, though, having dispatched five or so zombies that had wandered down the road in their absence. Soon, however, Justin was holding the lock in place as Patrick knocked the file deeper into the shackle.

"Whoa," Isherwood said, nudging the man with a booted foot. "This isn't a dude. It's a lady." The woman suddenly awoke with terror in her eyes, but fell helplessly into a coughing fit. They helped her to her feet and carried her outside to the trucks. Isherwood was excited to finally have an opportunity to use the survivor's kit he had put together for Old Blue. It had food and water, as well as some basic medical supplies.

They heard a door slam suddenly. Isherwood spun on his heels, dropping the kit and grabbing his gun. Justin and Patrick, too, nearly dropped the woman in favor of their sidearms. It was the boy they had found. After hiding timidly inside the Escalade the whole time, he was now running across the road to them without a fear in the world. He plowed right into the woman's legs. Patrick and Justin lowered her to the ground as she started to stir awake. There was dawning recognition on her face, though extremely weak. The boy immediately curled up in her lap, and she slowly reached up an arm to wrap around the boy. Isherwood pushed a bottle of water into her mouth, and she drank greedily from it.

"Not too much, not too much – it'll shock your system, ma'am."

"Momma, momma," they heard the boy whisper as he curled up against the woman's uniformed bosom. The three men looked at each incredulously. "Momma," the boy repeated.

"There's no way," Justin said. "That's just – just –"

"Yeah," Isherwood agreed. "Just that."

They helped the woman and the boy into the Escalade, and Justin agreed to sit with them while the other two finished searching the building for the weapons cache. It wasn't long before they found it. Luckily, the weapons area wasn't sealed like a bank vault. It was just another padlocked cage door that sealed off a windowless room. The padlock, however, hung open from the closed latch. Whoever had last emerged from the weapons locker had not been too concerned about sealing it back up.

"Wow," was all either of them could say for a minute, as their eyes darted around. There was some of everything in there and all of it in abundance. The pistol rack was knocked backwards and a pile of ammo lay scattered across the floor, but that was the only sign of the final struggle to take back the armory.

"It's like walking into an F.A.O. Schwartz," Patrick gurgled. There were racks and racks of 12 gauge tactical shotguns and M16 A4 automatic rifles, all with bayonets, tomahawks, frag and other kinds of grenades. There were M9 and M11 pistols in neat racks with stacks of ammunition lockers piled high around them.

"Or Wonka's Chocolate Room," Isherwood agreed. "There're actually *grenade launchers* in here, man. What the flip am I gonna do with one of those? Blow my head off, probably. But can you imagine? I could hold off thousands of those things from crossing the bridge. Or, the land bridges on either side of False River."

"How're we gonna get it all back to the church?" Patrick asked.

Isherwood laughed. "With glee."

CHAPTER SIXTEEN:
CARDINALS FANS

"I know you've been thinking about your family a lot," Isherwood said, interrupting himself as he droned on and on about his plans for St. Mary's. He and Sara were taking their morning stroll through the Prayer Garden, following morning coffee with Gran and the others. Sara had been giving him only short non-verbal replies for the last couple of minutes. Isherwood knew her attention lay elsewhere.

"My thoughts were that loud, huh?" Sara smiled sadly. "I've been trying really hard to keep that from you, because I knew there was enough on your shoulders already."

"I wish we could just get a message to them. I've been leaving cryptograms behind wherever we stop."

"Crypto-whats?"

"Just symbols spray-painted on the ground mostly that will tell only friendly people and family, I hope, where we are and not the thugs."

Sara was looking at Isherwood suspiciously, and not without a certain note of fear. "What symbol could do that?"

"It's a Chi-Rho pointing towards St. Mary's. I remembered that Christians in Rome used the Chi-Rho during the persecutions. It just blended in with the graffiti. Though," Isherwood added, looking a little worried, "mine won't be blending in with any graffiti."

"No," Sara said tugging on her husband's arm. "It's a brilliant idea, I'm sure. The bad guys will *definitely* not recognize that. But ..." she said, trailing off.

Isherwood had pulled her down to sit beside him on one of the garden benches. "Now what else did I do? Just yesterday, actually. We found a nicer radio. There was a UHF backpack radio in the armory. Vanessa was all wrapped around it. I think the solar-powered battery charger will charge its batteries. I think there's a working antenna, too. You can point it towards Whiskey Bay. I'll talk to Vanessa whenever she comes around."

Sara let out a sigh of relief. Isherwood could feel her shoulders heaving as she cried quietly in his arms. He was relieved for now that she was relieved. He knew, however, that whether or not the attempt to establish radio contact was successful, he would still need to figure out a way to get down to Whiskey Bay. He had already planned the route in his mind. He hadn't told Sara, but he guessed that she already knew.

*****

They had arrived back at St. Mary's an hour or so before sunset the night before. They were loaded down with the stockpile of weapons and their new guests. The men unloaded the weapons into a large closet in the St. Joseph Center, clearing out boxes of art and youth group supplies. Returning to the rectory for dinner, they found that the women had succeeded in nursing the black woman they had found back to consciousness. They had discovered that her name was Vanessa and that, despite the impossible odds, the boy they had also found that day was actually her son.

Wanting to give them space to recover, they had fixed up one of the offices in the church office as their bedroom. Isherwood was also glad they were not staying in the Rectory. He didn't know if either of them could yet be trusted following their traumatic experiences. It was still

120

possible, he thought, that either one of them could react violently to their new surroundings. He didn't particularly like his grandmother delivering their food alone. He had tried getting his Gran to change her mind once or twice before, which had been once or twice too many.

Gran had already delivered a couple trays of breakfast to their door that morning. She seemed to think they were still sleeping. Gran had flatly refused Isherwood, when he asked if he could maybe begin asking Vanessa questions. Gran again delivered trays of lunch to their door. She thought that the boy had probably awoken and then returned to sleep. His tray was licked clean, though his mother's remained untouched, except for the drink.

*****

That afternoon, they returned to the National Guard armory. They had apparently done away with most of the zombie population the day before. There were only a couple zombies for Old Blue to mow down. Isherwood and Justin were both riding in the backseat of the truck, following a protracted dispute about the rules of calling shotgun. Patrick was driving.

He drove them up close to the fenced-in parking lot behind the armory. Justin could almost break open the padlocked gate from the truck window. The top of the fence was lined with a coil of razor wire, and the parking lot was filled of an odd collection of vehicles, several of which were military. There was a small convoy of large, likely diesel trucks and troop transports, as well as two Humvees.

Once everybody and Old Blue were safely inside the fence, Isherwood said, "I say we take one of the big trucks and a Humvee, fill them up with diesel, and park them under cover in the pines by the Prayer Garden. They'll be our bug-out vehicles. Our 'exit strategy.' What d'you guys think?"

"Sounds good," Patrick said. "But where would we be bugging out *to?*"

Isherwood shrugged. "These things are like mobile shelters themselves. We could bug out into them until we find something that works."

"You sorta dodged the question there, buddy," Justin said turning to face Isherwood. "I know you've got not just one but a hundred ideas for locations in your head. What aren't you telling us?"

"It's the location I can't get out of my mind, because of Sara. It's probably a bad bug-out location to boot. It's Whiskey Bay." He took the next couple minutes explaining the situation to the other two. They each had family, too, that they would like to go searching for. They knew and expected Isherwood to realize as well that leaving to search for them would be too self-serving right now.

Patrick was reasoning with Isherwood, who was nodding in complete agreement. "You just can't direct *our* resources to a private mission. None of us can, just now. It would probably tear apart this little, fledgling community. And it's community keeping us alive."

"I agree. *Completely.*" Then, changing subjects, Isherwood began again. "I was actually thinking that right here – the armory – would make a great bug-out location. There are some old plantation homes I've been thinking about, too, for locations that are more out of the way."

The engine of the first truck wouldn't turn over, but the next one did. They were soon leaving the parking lot with a convoy of their own and headed back to LA Express to fill the tanks and the spare tanks of the vehicles with diesel fuel. Isherwood had read or saw on YouTube that diesel was less volatile than gasoline and so could be stored for a much longer time – probably why the Army used diesel in the first place, he thought. The diesel could just slosh around in the tanks until the vehicles were needed.

The LA Express down the eastern half of Main Street still seemed like the best place for hand-pumping, if only because it was near the Armory. The zombies Patrick had helped clear out the day before hadn't seemed to diminish the groups still staggering towards them.

Patrick had again parked Old Blue in the road in front of the station. "Does it seem to you," Isherwood was saying from the inside of the turret of the Humvee. Justin was taking the first turn at the hand pump today as penance for the Snickers debacle. Everybody would likely need to take a turn at the hand pump today, as there were probably over a hundred gallons of capacity in the two National Guard vehicles, given the spare tank on the truck. "Does it seem that more zombies are coming up from the direction of Waterloo?"

"Wouldn't know," Justin said breathlessly. "Just a pumping away down 'ere, sir."

"Yo, Patrick," Isherwood called, pointing east to Waterloo. "You seeing more coming from up that way?"

"You better believe it," Patrick called back emphatically. Isherwood felt like a rock had dropped into his stomach. Seeing Isherwood's skin pale, Patrick called out, "You think it's the bridge, don't you?"

Isherwood nodded gravely. "What're they looking like? Are their clothes shredded or torn off completely? Then, they're probably squeezing through the cracks we left for them. Not sure how, but whatever. Murphy's Law."

Patrick was slow to respond. He was looking through his scope, tediously studying the groups of twos and threes staggering down the road. "Yeah," he said pausing again. "Their clothes seem pretty messed up compared to others, but that's not it. There's something else."

Isherwood cocked an eyebrow as if something occurred to him for the first time. "Patrick?" he asked hesitantly, as though not truly wanting an answer to his question. "Are they ... soggy? You know, water-logged? Flesh like hanging from their necks and eye sockets?"

Patrick didn't say anything, but he lifted his head from the scope of the .22 and nodded gravely.

"Crap," Isherwood said shaking his head.

"Wait – what? I'm not getting it," Justin said, absent-mindedly cranking faster on the pump.

"I guess I had thought about it, but like a lot of other crap, I didn't *want* to think about it," Isherwood rambled. "It was just something I'd read in Max Brooks' book, back when zombies were still fiction. It seemed logical, but still far-fetched. He described swimmers getting pulled down and herds of those things roaming the ocean floor and huge groups of them just walking out of the surf on some random beach."

"What're you talking about, man?" Justin said, waving his free hand in frustration. "Spit it out."

"Exactly," Isherwood said, pointing at Justin with a touch of madness. "The River's just spitting them out. Zombies don't drown, but they're stupid enough to fall into water or get sucked up in the current chasing a rat or a sea gull. It's just like them crowding in for the static on the radio."

"So what?" Justin said cranking on the pump like he was a berserker. "If the zombies start falling off the Audubon bridge, they just float downstream – that's not *our* problem. They'd probably be almost to New Orleans before they popped back up again."

"Justin," Isherwood was saying with increasingly wilder eyes. "Then what's UP-stream from us?"

Justin fell quiet, but Isherwood was still winding up. "Everything, *every*-thing is upstream from us. We're sitting at the tail end of one of the biggest river systems in the world. The whole friggin' country might be flooding this way."

Patrick was stealing glances toward Isherwood, too, but Isherwood's steam was short-lived. He was winding down fast, as he saw the looks his friends were giving him. "Sorry," he said. "There's really not *that* much *immediately* upstream from us – Alexandria, Natchez, Vicksburg, maybe. It'll probably still be a long shot for us to starting seeing zombies washing up with Cardinals t-shirts, much less Reds or Twins or, God help us, Pirates." Isherwood soon fell quiet, though, as the conviction in his voice was quickly draining away.

"We'll figure this out, guys," he said sometime later. "Even if we have to line the levees with punji sticks. We'll figure it out. I promise. But let's not tell the others, just yet."

CHAPTER SEVENTEEN: BIRNAM WOOD

Old Blue, as well as the Jeep and the Escalade, were parked in a line along the River Road. All the vehicles had been modified by now with Jerry's help. The city maintenance shop, which Jerry and Isherwood had noticed during their first walkabout the church property, had proved extremely useful for all these modifications. Though the maintenance shed stood outside the church's fence, Jerry had modified and extended the shed's chain-link fence to provide a sturdy enough enclosure. The kids had started calling it Jerry's Place.

The vehicles were all blacked out with spray paint. A turret had been cut into the roofs of both the Escalade and the Jeep. Spare tires had been wrapped all around the vehicles. The vehicles all looked now like kids swimming on the lake with inner tubes wrapped around their bellies. Jerry had installed cattle grill guards which he then modified, as well. This made the trucks resemble locomotives, but they could now slice through a swarm of zombies like Moses through the Red Sea.

The Three Amigos, a name which had by now become permanent, were standing in the bed of Old Blue looking down the River Road and the long fence which ran along the base of the levees. The levees were high man-made mounds of dirt which ran for hundreds of miles along the sides of the Mississippi River. The Audubon Bridge stood not far in the distance, maybe a mile to the south.

"It looks like a Christo art installation," Isherwood said, piercing the quiet that had fallen on the three.

"A what?" Justin asked, distractedly.

"Just some super ultra-modern artist. He had these huge, like, environmental art works. Like *Running Fence,* which was just a long line – miles long – of white sheets stretching along the California coast. Or he'd have a never-ending line of flags standing in the desert or something. This just reminds me of that."

"I'd rather it remind you of a brilliant battle plan of Patton's or something," Patrick said. "Christo was weird."

They were staring in horror at the long fence line straddling the base of the levee for miles and miles into the distance. It was barbed wire, as cattle once grazed up and down the levees. The barbed wire looked, as Isherwood had described, as though someone had come and hung thousands of ragged flags along the fence. The tatters of clothing left hanging on the fence were all different colors, but mostly dark red.

"This is the worst section of fence we've yet seen," Justin said, still staring. They had been driving along and surveying the twenty or so miles of the River Road that stood along the backside of St. Maryville, from one end of False River to the other.

"Yeah," Isherwood nodded. "Right here, this is a bend in the river. The current probably does something weird in all the turbulence and flushes them up onto the banks. Who knows?"

"Ok, sure," Patrick said, looking around into the open farmland and pastures beyond the fence on the opposite side of the road. The open land ended in thick woods about three hundred yards from the road. "But where did they all go? Why are they climbing up the levees and why aren't they here? Where the heck did they go?"

Both Justin and Isherwood just shrugged.

"I don't know," Isherwood finally said. "But if there gets to be too many of them, we're gonna have to do our zombie conga line all over again."

"But probably not over the bridge again," Justin said.

"No, you're right," Isherwood agreed, "but we still need to seal up the gaps on either side of False River."

Patrick sighed. "Unless your whole concept of the Mississippi and False River being natural barriers is disproven now."

"Man, there was a time when I would've flown off the handle for that, for you accusing me of being wrong. Times sure have changed, though. There's that at least. I hate it, Patrick, but you're probably right. Even if I'm not *completely* wrong, the plan just might not be as practical or as profitable as before."

"Hell, holy hell!" Patrick suddenly cried out. "Look! Birnam Wood comes now to high Dunsinane."

"Oh God," Isherwood said. For a moment he just closed his eyes, trying to check out. He couldn't do it. "Come on, Justin. Let's get in our own vehicles, so they'll have to swarm all of us. In fact, let's spread out a bit if we can. That fence will give us some time. This must've been what Cemetery Ridge felt like when Pickett's grey soldiers started marching out of the woods."

"Dang," Justin said, "Just dang."

As they watched sidelong, running back to their cars, it seemed like a near solid line of zombies was emerging from the woods three hundred yards in front of them, on the opposite side of the road from the levee. There were hundreds and more still were emerging. The men had clearly been sighted because they could hear the first stirrings of moaning. It chilled them down to the soles of their feet. It was guttural and primitive, but with terrible vestiges of humanity. The sound was echoing through the woods. They were calling to each other. Wave upon wave of the sound began receding backward, deeper and deeper into the woods. There was no telling how many had been drawn over the levee and into the woods. Flocks of birds started erupting here and there from the treetops, like something massive was tearing through the woods.

Justin and Isherwood soon emerged from the hatches newly cut into the rooves of their SUVs. Isherwood was signaling the church on the radio, giving them their location and describing the situation. "Whatever you do, please do not leave the church to try and rescue us." He repeated. "Stay put, we'll be fine." He wanted to tell them to give a message to Sara and his kids, to tell them he loved them, but he knew it would cause panic.

"Guys," Justin called to Patrick ahead of him in Old Blue and Isherwood behind him in the Jeep. "Angle your vehicles towards the fence, or else they might tip us right over. You gotta paddle into the wave!"

They were soon in position. The first wave was still a hundred yards away, while the main body was still two hundred yards off.

"Y'all know how I hate wasting bullets," Isherwood called out as he went to stand along the fence line with a Bowie knife in either hand. "I'll take care of this first wave. Y'all start working on the bigger group behind them."

"You got it, buddy," Justin called out. Patrick chose to answer with bullets, waiting until the next group had advanced to around seventy-five yards.

Ten or so hit the fence at once. Isherwood dispatched the first five or so quickly, since they were right on him. The other half were about ten yards further down the fence. By the time he had run down to them, only one had been able to spill over the fence. Isherwood stabbed this one while its skull was still stuck in the mud of the ditch. The rest were busy relieving themselves of whatever bowels they had left after the first two times they had slogged over the barbed wire. Isherwood tried not to look down at the wings of flesh that still flapped down from their rib cages immodestly shielding the empty caverns where once sagged the zombie's bloated bellies. "Hell," he yelled. "I just saw straight down into that thing's pelvis."

"Pervert!" Justin yelled back, after blowing off the back of a skull from eighty yards.

Isherwood stole a glance every ten seconds or so towards the main group of zombies. He was also trying to figure out how deep this group was still emerging from the forest. From his angle on the ground, he couldn't tell. "They still coming out of the woods? How's it looking?" he called back to Justin and Patrick.

"Dude, you don't want to know," Patrick replied, as he was reloading.

"We're starting to build a nice little mound of bodies at about seventy-five yards, though," Justin added. "Dead heads keep tripping over themselves."

"Nice, man." Isherwood called back without turning from the fence. He hit three in a row without having any issues getting the blade back out of the skull. The bone was soft from being submerged so long.

"Just call me 'Z-wall Jackson'," Justin said, laughing at himself.

Patrick called out from behind Isherwood. "Get a look at this fella. My side, maybe ten yards in. Ever seen something like that? Shoot."

Isherwood pulled himself from the fence to get a look at what Patrick was pointing at. He took the chance to wipe his face. At about ninety yards, they saw a zombie whose torso was bending at a grisly angle. Most of its right side was missing. It looked like he had been clipped by a giant hole puncher.

"Bet it was one of those Mississippi bull sharks," Patrick yelled over the sound of gunfire.

"Or one big-arse catfish," Justin called back.

"Crap," Isherwood said as he lunged ten yards north along the fence. There were eight zombies about to fall forward over the top wire of the fence. He was yelling at them, "Come on you filthy, zed heads, drag yourselves along that fence." He was hoping the zombies would snag an exposed rib or sheet of flesh along the wire as they dragged themselves against it. He was playing a dangerous game, though. He knew the wire would eventually snap if enough bodies leaned against it or on top of it. If the fence lines did snap, the steep-sided ditch still stood between them and the advancing horde.

He succeeded in stalling the eight zombies long enough to stab through the sides of their skulls. It would not be much longer, he noticed, until the top line of barbed wire was perfectly smooth. Gore, filth, and entrails were slowly coating it, rendering the barbs useless.

Justin and Patrick had thinned the main body of zombies significantly, so that the main body appeared for a moment to be retreating. The pace of the zombies throwing themselves against the fence was still slowly increasing, however. For now, Isherwood was keeping pace, walking up and down the line delivering death as at Hell's own communion rail.

He thanked God that his clothes – his sleeves, gloves, and even a face mask were all Army issue now – were holding up. The zombies, even the falling ones, were still grabbing at him and scratching. It wasn't just gnarled fingernails. Most of the zombies lacked the flesh at the fingertips altogether. It was the sharp tips of bones protruding from the ends of their fingers that dug the deepest.

"Ding!" Isherwood called out. He had just finished a long run of zombies, tapping their skulls with his knife like a long line of typewriter keys. "How's the ammo supply?" Isherwood called back to Justin and Patrick.

"I've got another 500 rounds. I could do this all night," Justin said leaning over the butt of his rifle. "Just found a comfortable position, too."

"Yeah, I've got a little less," Patrick answered. "But that's not even counting the automatic rifles we've got stashed away."

"I'm about to switch to my pistol." Isherwood advised them. "These things are starting to mound up against the fence. I can see it starting to lean. Any end in sight?"

"From the trees directly ahead of us, yeah," Patrick answered. "But the arrow point is starting to broaden at the base. Know what I mean?"

"No real end in sight, then?" Isherwood asked rhetorically. "Well, we better pack it in before the fence gives way. But first, how about y'all get down here and we go full auto for a bit. What d'you say?"

"I say that sounds excellent," Justin said, before the words had even escaped Isherwood's mouth. He was already standing beside Isherwood. "May I?" he said stepping in front of Isherwood.

"Be my guest," Isherwood said, stepping back and taking the opportunity to catch his breath. He noticed that Justin was leveling the same AR-15 rifle he had brandished the day they reunited on Major Parkway. He had a second one slung across his back. "Been waiting for this, have you?"

"Hells yeah," he said. Despite the difficulty aiming the automatic weapon, Justin was mowing down the zombies, head shot after head shot after head shot.

"That's not even fair," Isherwood said as Justin slammed in a fresh magazine. "You've got a second semi-circular mound forming up perfectly, too. The fence will be just fine." He called up to Patrick, who was still working on building up the first mound at seventy-five yards. "Hey, any sign of Z's coming down the road?"

"Hot dog!" Patrick called out, as he suddenly redirected his rifle to the few zombies ambling up the boulevard. "Got 'em. You may return to your affairs."

"Be right back," Isherwood said, as he left Justin and crossed the ditch back to his Jeep. With just his pistols, he was having trouble with accuracy at the new range Justin had established with the AR. He re-holstered his 9mm's – he had upgraded to a pair of them – and grabbed a pair of A4s from the gun racks they had installed inside the back of the Jeep.

"I'll get this half, brother," Isherwood called over to Justin as he was re-crossing the ditch. "We may be able to finish this fight after all, now that the new mound is keeping them off the fence." Isherwood was beginning to think that the mounds they were building could be the beginning of a long line of grisly fortifications, built out of the enemy, itself.

"Ah yeah, man," Justin said, finishing off another mag. "This is just pure stress-relief now. Let's wait until either the sun sets behind the wall of the dead or else we blot out of the sun itself."

They didn't quite make it to sundown, as Justin had hoped. When the flow of zombies finally diminished to a trickle, Patrick had nearly run out of ammunition for his .22 rifle. If he had not had a second .22, the first would have burned through his gloved hands long before the end. Altogether, Patrick reckoned he had shot nearly 600 zombies. Patrick's mound stretched out a radius of about seventy or eighty yards, sweeping the full one hundred eighty degrees from north to south. The mound Justin had started and Isherwood had contributed to swept out the same arc at twenty yards. The two lines of semi-circles were nearly perfectly concentric.

"Wow, that Christo guy's got nothing on us," Justin was laughing. He was standing at the back of the Escalade re-filling his emptied magazines and admiring their handiwork. "Better radio the church, or they'll think we're goners."

Isherwood was soon on the radio, thankful for Justin's reminder. He was kicking himself for not remembering to check in. "This is Isherwood, over." There was no return transmission. Just silence. "Isherwood, over," he repeated. He didn't wait for another round of silence.

"Guys, let's move," he called out his window as he passed the Escalade and then Old Blue. "There's no answer on the radio."

CHAPTER EIGHTEEN: BOXED-OFF

The three vehicles led by Old Blue immediately started honking when they pulled within sight of St. Mary's. As they came down Main Street from the east, fresh from fighting the "River Dead" as they would later be called, they immediately saw that trouble was brewing. They had been unable to hear the moans over the sound of the engines. Old Blue stopped in the center of the intersection of Main and New Roads Streets. The one stoplight in what amounted to downtown St. Maryville was hanging just above their heads. Isherwood passed up Justin in the Escalade and pulled alongside of Old Blue. Taking the cue, Justin pulled up along the right side of Old Blue. This created an instant barricade across most of Main Street.

"I get why they weren't answering the radio," Isherwood said as he emerged from the homemade turret of the Jeep.

Justin was grumbling complaints as he and Patrick also emerged from the holes in the roofs of their vehicles. "Dang, man. I was not emotionally prepared for this tonight. A bath, yes – another blood bath, no."

Isherwood was still managing to reach the steering wheel horn with his long legs. He couldn't see through the crowd of zombies to inside the fence. The mass was just too thick. "I bet Sara and our wives are just inside the fence, working the line with knives."

"Yeah," Patrick said. "The 'dead' zombies are starting to pile up. If the mound gets much higher the zombies will just walk right over the fence." He was starting to panic, Justin and Isherwood could hear it in his voice.

"Patrick, how's your ammo supply?" Isherwood asked to distract his friend. He bet that Sara was fighting those things and was too busy to answer their radio calls. She probably also thought that the surest, fastest way to get the men home was to *not* answer the radio.

"It's not good," Patrick answered. "My .22s are almost completely out, and I'm betting Justin's automatics are pretty well spent."

"I've probably got the best supply," Isherwood answered, passing a package of 500 .22 caliber rounds to each of them. "Let's turn on our lights. This could go past sunset. And let's build a wall of dead across Main Street, what d'you say? It could prove useful. If not, Jerry's tractor can just bulldoze them into a bonfire."

Justin and Patrick didn't answer, but immediately disappeared back into their vehicles to turn on their headlamps. "Okay, where do you want to draw the line?" Patrick asked, when he re-emerged from Old Blue's turret. "From Roy's Jewelry Shop straight across to whatever that building is called. It's pretty close to us, maybe only twenty yards, but we shouldn't miss even in the dark and I think we're pretty solid inside our trucks."

"Wouldn't mind having the Humvee just now, though," Justin said and then added, "Good plan. I like it."

"Still, I'm glad our families have access to those National Guard vehicles. Though I'm pretty much freaking out – it doesn't look like those creeps have yet gotten around the back side. If they needed to get out, they could've and still could. Let's do this, though. Nobody messes with my family."

Their arrival and incessant honking was doing the trick. They were beginning to turn heads. It still took another two or three minutes for the first zombies to reach the twenty yard line they had marked out in their minds. By that time, Justin had begun taking long range shots. "What?" he said indignantly, "My finger was getting itchy."

"It's cool, dude. It'll help them hustle. Just don't drop them along the fence."

"Nowhere close to the fence, *please*." Isherwood said with irritation. "The only bad part about this plan is that the backstop for our bullets isn't far off from our families. A ricochet could be *really* bad. In fact," he said reaching down to grab a radio. "Hey, can someone pick up a radio, please? We're here and we're drawing them our way, but we need y'all to hide, so they'll lose interest in you, and take cover indoors, so our bullets don't accidentally hit you. Over? *Click-shhh*."

A second later the radio hummed to life. "About time y'all showed up!" Isherwood was relieved to hear Sara's voice on the other end. He let out a long breath he hadn't even realized he was holding. "The fences are solid. Robert, on those instructions. *Click-shhh.*"

Isherwood looked puzzled, and then started laughing. "Oh! You mean 'Roger' – like Roger Workman. Good. Love you, love to all. Over and out. *Click-shhh.*"

"Man," Patrick said. "I didn't realize how complacent I'd become with their safety. That ends tonight," he said. Isherwood was glad to see Patrick's changed attitude and that he was responding with renewed energy and not resignation. He was actually more worried about Justin, who seemed to be remaining on the sarcastic side of his personality with very few ripples of change. He was also worried about his family being distracted and alone with Vanessa and her boy, who were both still unknowns as mental health went. He pushed all this out of his mind for now. It was time for shooting.

They divided up the road into left, middle, and right, though Justin was eating up the middle right, as well. "Oh, dang," Patrick said, pulling the trigger. "That was Ms. Mary Allen. She taught in the elementary."

"Well, buddy. She's coming after your kids now," Justin replied.

"She *was*, anyway," Patrick answered.

The line of bodies didn't really start stacking up until they had downed around thirty or so zombies. After that, it became easier. The line of corpses became clearer, and the zombies slowed significantly as they staggering from the even road and started stumbling. It became more difficult when they fell, because they fell out of sight of the scopes. They quickly learned to sweep left and right at crawl, stoop, and full upright heights.

As the sun began setting behind the growing mound of corpses, the light from the truck headlamps began playing tricks with the zombie's eyes. Sometimes the eyes would glow red. "I've gotta a pinko," Justin shouted over the bursts of gunfire. "Like an albino bunny."

"Whoa!" Isherwood shouted.

"I know, right?" Justin said laughing with a screech.

"No, not that," Isherwood answered. "I've got some zeds at my jeep." The other two stopped firing and looked down and around them in surprise. There weren't many, but, sure enough, they were getting flanked. "Patrick," Isherwood said. "You stay on the church crowd. Justin, can you cover up New Roads Street and I'll get the things behind us?"

They were parked in a 'T' intersection. Main Street crossed through and New Roads Street ended in a parking lot to the side of Roy's Jewelry Shop. The parking lot continued back dropping off sharply into sort of a driveway-alley that led down to the riverfront. The parking lot was on Isherwood's side and there was no z-action on that side.

"Sure, boss," Justin answered gruffly, imitating some kind of bruiser character from a mobster movie. "Hey, try starting lines like we got in front of us, okay? We'll make a box. Get it?"

"Got it," Isherwood answered. Before they started trying to mound up zombies up New Roads Street and back east on Main Street toward the courthouse, they had to clear out the ones that were right on them.

"You little punk," Justin said under his breath, as he reached over and stabbed a zombie in the head. It was scratching unfleshed fingertips along the roof of the Escalade towards him, but couldn't get anywhere close. The spare tires they had mounted on the sides of the vehicles forced the zombies to keep their distance.

"Hey," Patrick turned to ask. "Was it an RD?"

Justin looked at him funny. "Huh?"

"You know, an RD – a 'River Dead.' Was it water-logged?"

"Oh, I don't know," Justin answered. "But yeah, I'd say probably yeah."

"*Crap*," Isherwood cursed, as Patrick shook his head.

Justin paused a second from shooting up New Roads Street. There was a break in the zombies, anyway. "Look, guys. We'll take care of it. This new tactic is working awesome. These trucks are taking care of business. And look, we're about to finish up here, anyway."

As Justin pointed, Patrick noticed that nearly all the zombies had left the church fence and the lines toward the growing mound were slackening.

"Sure," Isherwood agreed. "But we don't want to run out of bullets before the river runs out of dead."

To see that the tide of zombies coming at them from the church was slackening, Justin had needed to pull himself up out of the turret of his vehicle. The barricade of zombie corpses had risen up quickly. It was now about as high as Old Blue's cab, though it was much thicker in the middle of the road than at the sides.

"Hey, guys," Patrick called out over the hail of gunfire. "Can you switch directions with me? They're starting to come around the sides more and more now that the middle is so high." Justin and Isherwood switched without another word.

"We're looking good down here," Sara's voice came over the radios. "Whatever y'all are doing is working fine. Dinner's waiting for you whenever you finish. *Click-shhh.*"

"Heard that," Isherwood laughed. Loud enough to be heard over the rifles, Justin's belly roared at the mention of dinner.

"Hey, guys?" Patrick asked, alternately facing east along Main and north along New Roads Street. "I like the boxed in approach, but how're we getting out of here? We've blocked off all the roads!"

CHAPTER NINETEEN: THE ABBOT'S VISION

The three men managed to finally return to the church grounds, albeit covered in gunpowder and with their ears still ringing. They had clunked their way through a gap in one of the corpse walls. The New Roads Street wall was still thin enough at the edges for the trucks to pass through. The cattle grill guards that Uncle Jerry had installed were coming in really handy.

Sara greeted them at the back gate, the same one they had passed through when they first arrived at the church nearly a week ago. When they got back to the Rectory, everyone was there to welcome them back. There was also a hot meal waiting for them.

Vanessa and her boy were there to greet them, as well. The boy's name, it turned out, was Le'Marcus. Isherwood was relieved at their mental state, which appeared as good as could be expected. Vanessa was still twitchy, but seemed friendly enough. He knew that black girls were the toughest babies, the most likely to survive when born premature. Black women were probably just as tough, he thought. Vanessa gave each of the men a hug to show her gratitude. They all agreed afterwards that she must not have lost any muscle mass. Justin added, "I think that hug cracked a rib." They were all glad, especially Isherwood, that not only had they found survivors and not only for them, miraculously, being mother and son, but that they looked to become very productive members of the community. Isherwood decided an in-depth conversation with Vanessa about radios could wait until the morning.

"Steak with a side of steak for our men," Sara had said. Justin was especially grateful for the meal. They hadn't realized how hungry and weary they had become. The sustained adrenaline rushes of the day had left their hands shaking. They finished their meal quickly and were soon led to bed by their wives. To a man, they fell asleep before their heads even hit their pillows.

*****

The next morning following Morning Prayer everybody was in the Rectory dining room for breakfast. Monsignor was seated at the head of the table. The rest of the men, except for Jerry, had elected to let the women sit in their places at the table. Isherwood was leaning against the mantelpiece, while Emma and Charlie ate at his feet at a little table that had been brought over from the Sunday school room. Sara was drinking a second cup of coffee at his side.

Isherwood was explaining what they had seen the day before, telling them about the fence lines covered in tattered rags and the river dead. Justin and Patrick added details here and there. "I'm not saying we should expect to have z-guests at our front gates every day, but it could happen. We've got plenty of ammo for now, but it can't last forever unless we start manufacturing our own, reusing our casings. But even then, there are other limiting factors like gunpowder. We can use knives, spears, swords and the like to kill them at the fence, but in a prolonged fight they could mound up high enough and just start spilling over the top of the fence. Even then, we'll need Jerry on the tractor regularly clearing away the mounds from the fence. We'd need a massive zombie landfill slash mass burial site. Or else, maybe we could start using the corpses as fortifications. Here's where I stand. Let's see how things go over the next week. If the numbers keep increasing, we'll move on to greener pastures. If not, it may have just been a freak belching of dead out of the river."

"Belching, really?" Justin laughed. Isherwood winked at him, but the room soon fell silent.

Finally, Monsignor spoke up. "Isherwood, that sounds like a fine plan. Just keep us updated daily – after breakfast is a good time, just not while we're *eating*." He smiled at his joke to help lighten the mood in the room.

Monsignor next asked for updates on their food supplies from Gran and Tad who were in charge of the pantry. The Three Amigos' subsequent raids on Langlois' grocery had mostly emptied the store. Gran and Tad believed they had salvaged and preserved almost all of the meat using a brine solution, and were ready to process what Patrick had stored temporarily in brine inside Wal-Mart. They had also converted the large front room of the St. Joseph Center into a massive pantry. They had salvaged cinder blocks and wood planks from here and there to make aisles of shelves. They had managed to turn the pantry into what resembled a little grocery store stacked high with glass jars of salvaged fruits and vegetables, bags of rice and grain, and all the other goods that had been brought in through the raids.

Isherwood asked Gran and Tad whether, if they had the time, they could also organize the armory. He was hoping to add to it soon with raids on the sheriff's and police stations. They hadn't yet had the time to organize it after unloading it all from the National Guard outpost. The old supply closet of the St. Joseph Center was a good space, but it would soon become a disaster. A good inventory was also desperately needed, if they didn't mind, Isherwood added.

Jerry gave an update on the fields he'd planted. He had been given bags of potatoes from Wal-Mart and Langlois' that had started sprouting. With the help of Patrick and Justin's kids and, of course, the new tractor, they had planted almost 3,000 feet of potato rows. Jerry wasn't too sure about the seed corn he had planted. He'd know more by next week, he said, guessing that everything ought to be sprouting by then. He also mentioned that the old well on the property, as well as the pump, were still functioning. It would be ready to go when or if the water pressure finally failed.

Sara had taken charge of the gardens, along with Denise and Chelsea, Patrick and Justin's wives, respectively. They had taken the huge National Guard truck out to Tractor Supply and loaded it down with all the seeds and poultry feed they could find.

"You did what?" Isherwood asked, taken completely aback. He had no idea that anyone besides he, Patrick, and Justin had been making raids. Sara explained that they had been very safe.

"Almost all the mothers could've been wiped out at once," Isherwood stammered. "And who of you knew how to drive that big old truck?"

"I did," said Chelsea to Justin's great surprise. Chelsea smiled at her husband's discomfort. "Used to date a guy that drove big rigs," she explained.

"Okay, I'm glad y'all did it and got back safe," Isherwood went on. "But, at least until we can figure out the extent of the – of the infestation, nobody leaves except for the three of us. *And,* nobody leaves *at all* without letting us know. We've got to be able to coordinate our movements. Everybody understand?"

Sara reluctantly agreed to hold off for now. "Besides," she said. "We've got more than enough to occupy us right here for now." She went on to explain that they had also taken the store's entire stock of Greenhouses-In-A-Box. They had assembled three 10 foot by 20 foot greenhouses on the large back parking lot to start making use of all the unusable concrete space, as well as another two, smaller greenhouses in the parking lot along the west side of the church grounds.

With the help of Jerry's tractor, they had also tilled up the lawns along the eastern side of the church. They were still waiting for their seedlings to sprout in the greenhouses, but they had already built wire trellises to grow bush beans and tomatoes. They were going to start converting the flower beds around the church office and between and around the rest of the buildings into vegetable beds. They would use the walls of the buildings to support tall plants and trellises.

The ladies were also looking towards building and scouting out fruit orchards. They had a number of fruit trees they planned to plant up and down the rectory's large front lawn. Sara asked if the raiding parties could start filling in a map that she had with the various orchards around the parish and within the city, itself. Isherwood was really excited at this idea and eagerly took the map, which Sara had already begun filling in from memory. He knew, too, that the long plots of land around town were full of pecan tree orchards, and that the protein found in the nuts could serve as a protein substitute if their supplies of meat were to dwindle.

Monsignor seemed to have followed a similar train of thought. "If I may interrupt, I would like for this group to begin thinking towards how we could conserve the cattle population in the area. I believe, though I do not know, that most of the cattle around here will be able to sustain themselves without much help from us. The grass is growing fast and the rains should provide plenty of drinking water. Once the summer is upon us, however, the cattle will need our help. I understand that we won't be able to save all the cattle – not even close – but we can scout out the best pasture land and bring what's left of the cattle populations there. Isherwood, am I right to believe that some cattle remain despite those creatures attacking them?"

Isherwood nodded, looking to Patrick and Justin for confirmation. "Oh sure, Monsignor. They're definitely an endangered species, but we're still seeing them here and there. The herds along the levees are all but gone, but the ones in pastures with better fencing have fared much better."

"I've actually seen a cow charge and stomp a zombie," Patrick said. "A small herd of cows could easily defend themselves against one or two zombies."

"That's fine," Monsignor nodded. "Please start with the cattle, gentlemen, but I would also like to see us round up as many of the domesticated animals as we can. We have some chickens and ducks from the Smith family. Horses, I'm sure, will also become more and more useful as our gas supplies begin to evaporate. Perhaps you could start pulling trailers behind your trucks to start collecting what you can. Cages, as well." Monsignor stopped. "Isherwood, is everything okay?"

"Oh, yeah, Monsignor," he nodded heartily. "I just can't believe what we're doing here. It's amazing. Everybody is *really* coming together. I had been feeling so overwhelmed with ideas for things that needed to be done. And now, this morning, as I've been listening, y'all have been rattling off every one of them. It's not aspirations or plans, either – it's stuff you've *already* accomplished. It's just incredible. I'm so proud of everybody." Sara had sidled up next to him and was hugging him around the waist. There were tears in her eyes.

"I think that is owed in no small part to you, Isherwood. Your own inspiration and enthusiasm is, well, infectious." Monsignor smiled warmly at the younger man. "So, yes, in a time when we ought to be, by all odds, thinking of merely staying alive, we've all come together to form a much bigger picture. On that note, I'd also like for us to start thinking *even* bigger, beyond St. Maryville and the parish, beyond our little island kingdom. I have no doubt that God intends for us to think towards bringing back civilization, itself." He let his words sink in, before he went on.

"All of you, remember this – humanity has been brought to the brink many times before this. As recently as the Middle Ages, the bubonic plague – the Black Death, as it was called – literally decimated Europe's population. It killed a third of the continent's population and took the world hundreds of years to recover. Now, I have no doubt that this disaster is global and has cut far deeper into the world's population. Perhaps our species has never before been so close to extinction since the days of Noah."

"When civilization roared back out of the so-called Dark Ages following the collapse of the Roman Empire, how did it happen?" Monsignor looked from face to face. "Isherwood? How did it happen?"

"The monasteries," he answered. Monsignor nodded for him to go on. "Agriculture," Isherwood said, picking up steam. "The monks, they pretty much rearranged the countryside of Europe, draining swamps, redirecting rivers. They became especially good at cultivating wine for the sacraments. Dom Perignon invented champagne, too. They built massive walled monasteries. There was Cluny in France that became just massive. Monks from Cluny farmed a vast section of Europe, I think."

"That's right," Monsignor said, tapping his hand on the table like a gavel. "And I think a similar model would work for us."

"I'm gonna be a monk?" Justin interrupted, incredulously.

"More like a Friar Tuck," Patrick answered. Everybody cracked up at this. Even Justin nodded in agreement.

"Okay, yeah," Justin agreed. "I can get behind this. I was going bald on top anyway."

Monsignor raised a hand, still laughing. "Now, I said a *similar* model could work for us. I think a solid core of priests would be a strong foundation for us, but obviously married couples would be needed because almost all of you are and we have to work towards restoring the population. A solid core of priests could help us as *missionaries.*"

"This is why I'd like us to keep searching for survivors," Monsignor went on. "But we need to look beyond our parish. I believe we will soon resolve our 'infestation' issues, as Isherwood described them. I believe these will be only temporary setbacks. Once our borders are secure, we will start planning longer range expeditions. It will be more dangerous. *Much* more so."

"Monsignor," Isherwood said, feeling Sara's arm tighten his lungs. "I would go wherever you told me, but I'm worried about leaving my family behind."

"I know you would," Monsignor answered. "But you're right. We'll need more men. This is why I'm asking you to go to on a couple mid-range raids. First, I want you to go to Morganza. I have a very strong feeling that Father Simeon has survived. He may even have a group with him, like us, there behind the fences of St. Anne's. Also, I hope that you, Vanessa, will be able to help us. I understand that you are very good with a radio."

Everybody turned to Vanessa and Le'Marcus, who no one but Monsignor had noticed come down the hallway and join them. They saw the woman was nodding eagerly.

Isherwood and the men were nodding, too, excited at the prospect of survivors. "That'll be our top priority, Monsignor," Patrick said, speaking for the others. "Just as soon as we get a handle on the RDs. That's what we're calling the 'River Dead,' I mean."

There were a few more odds and ends to address before the morning's meeting ended. Monsignor finally closed the meeting, himself. "Today," he announced, "is actually Sunday. Did anyone know that? I think it's been a full week since Isherwood's crew arrived. Doesn't it feel like it was a world ago?"

The table murmured in appreciation for the time that had passed and what they had managed to accomplish.

"Since it is Sunday, I would like all of you to join me for Mass. Jerry and Tad, I think you're non-denominational, isn't that right? But you were raised Catholic?"

Caught off guard, Tad was speechless and Jerry hadn't heard the old priest anyway. Tad just nodded.

"Well, then, I think it's time you came back to the church." Monsignor had said it in his way, both gentle and firm, but the statement was somehow beyond questioning. "Vanessa and Le'Marcus – you, too. It's about 10:45 now. I'll be starting at 11 o'clock, though I always do start a little late," he laughed. "The priests around here call me the 'Late' Monsignor Robert Bellarmine."

"Now," he continued once the laughter subsided. "All you coffee drinkers have broken fast, but that will be alright. We'll do better next time. Come as you are. The kids are welcome in their pajamas. Isherwood, though, you better change that sweatshirt," Monsignor said, laughing. Isherwood, too, was laughing. He was wearing his faded and somewhat tattered college sweatshirt, which was fine, except that the grey sweatshirt did not read "LSU".

145

CHAPTER TWENTY:
HERD

The Three Amigos stayed put on the church grounds Sunday afternoon. Justin called it a day of rest, but they didn't want to leave just yet. They didn't want to leave their families and home base just yet if another wave of RDs were about to swarm the church grounds. Isherwood watched from the church's bell tower most of the day. Fortunately and amazingly, the downtown zombie population had diminished to almost nothing. Even if recurring, the problem of the River Dead, Isherwood hoped, might be only sporadic.

Sara had climbed up the bell tower to sit with him and watch the sun set. She brought her compound bow with her, too, just in case. She was rarely ever without it these days. She said it was just a good habit to grow accustomed to carrying it.

"I've been thinking about the River Dead – the 'RD' – problem," Isherwood said. "Maybe you could help me brainstorm. I've been trying to thing how we could use our little cage idea."

"To distract them?" Sara asked, leaning her head against his chest.

"Right, to distract them back towards the river, just far enough for the tide to drag them back in."

"The tide *is* incredibly strong," Sara agreed. "It wouldn't take much. They're not exactly steady on their feet."

"Yeah, and if not something simple like that, we might as well build walls atop the levees. We just don't have the manpower for that – and the *fuel*. Can you imagine the gas we'd burn? Even if we did short lengths of walls in just the hot spots, it would take forever."

"So, you'd have a cage actually *in* the river? Like an animal floating in a barge anchored in place somehow? What kind of animal would survive? Even some kind of noisemaker would eventually get dragged under or somehow destroyed."

"Well, we're not short on stuff anymore," Isherwood was saying. "We could anchor whole tugboats or something out there. We could triple anchor it or something."

"But what could stay alive out there indefinitely? Could you rig up something that caught fish and water to feed a little flock of chickens, maybe?"

"Yeah, that's the trouble. How to build these things to last without constant monitoring? We don't have the manpower for that."

"Well," Sara said. "We might if it served a double purpose. I could see somebody going out a couple times a week to check trotlines. They could just toss the bad fish to the chickens, like hardhead catfish, and bring back the blues and channel cats. Probably some giant sac-au-lait, too. Bluegill. Giant everything, really."

"That's brilliant, Mrs. Smith," he said, squeezing her. "We could rig up a chicken coop on a boat easy, I bet. Cover the thing in chicken wire. If we had a tug, we could store the water in the cabin to reduce evaporation and maybe rig it up with rain barrels."

"This might actually be a great way to raise chickens, too!" she said growing excited.

Isherwood was laughing, "River chickens! Probably the first time anyone's ever had a chicken farm on water. We could rig up trot lines clear across the river, I guess. Not too much traffic these days. It'll probably be easier just to keep to the sides, maybe even some jug-fishing.

We'll have to figure out how to dry and preserve fish – we need to build a *smoke house*."

"The Pilot Channel by Whiskey Bay is really good for trotlines," Sara said. Isherwood noticed the abrupt change in his wife's tone as her thoughts turned to her family. It wasn't long before the tears began.

He took her by the shoulders so he could look right into her down-turned face. "That's the very next trip we're making after Morganza. Oh my God, honey – of course it will be. We're *almost* there!" Sara breathed a heavy sigh and smiled. She settled back under his arm. "We're setting out for Morganza bright and early tomorrow morning, too. Won't it be nice to have Father Simeon here? And then we'll be off to Whiskey Bay. Everything's falling into place, I promise."

*****

As promised, the three men left early the next morning. Each vehicle was now stocked with a group raiding kit, as well as a backpack for each person stuffed tight with an individual survival kit. The group raiding kit included, in addition to the large armory of guns, ammunition, and explosives stored in each vehicle, the following: a medical kit; an axe and a hatchet; two pairs of bolt cutters; two crowbars; a tool kit with pliers, screwdrivers, and saws; two rolls of duct tape; several hundred feet of rope and two grappling hooks, either just hook and rope or Army-issue LGHs; an extension ladder; digging tools; two sets of binoculars; three milk jugs of drinking water; compasses; a local and a regional map; a radio and extra batteries; and emergency flares.

The individual kits included, besides a primary and secondary firearm and fifty rounds of ammo for each, the following: a sanitation kit, a Nalgene bottle filled with about a quart of water, knife, a signaling mirror, a flashlight and radio with extra batteries, a hand-to-hand weapon, some flares, matches stored in a Ziploc bag, five Power Bars, boots, and fresh socks.

Old Blue was again at the head of their company as they set out through the northwest gate of the church yard. Isherwood rode along with Patrick in Old Blue, and Justin followed behind them in his Escalade. They had hitched a horse trailer to the back of Old Blue to pick up any cattle they might happen upon.

They had decided with Monsignor's blessing that the threat from the river had been eliminated enough for now. Besides, Morganza was not much farther from the center of town than Waterloo was. They weren't sure why they hadn't made the trip sooner, except that there wasn't much to find in the small town besides survivors.

They again took Major Parkway to get to the back of town while avoiding Hospital Road. They stopped at the gas station at the end of Hospital Road where Isherwood had drawn the symbol across the concrete. There were steady waves of zombies coming at them, but nothing to compare with the River Dead from the other day. Patrick took a turn at the hand pump and they topped off their gas tanks. They hadn't used much gas over the course of the week. At their current rate of consumption, it would take over a month to empty their tanks.

They stalled before leaving town and laid on their horns, hoping to draw as many zombies westward away from town as possible. They drove slowly, never exceeding thirty miles per hour. The Morganza Highway, as it was called, followed roughly the same route upriver as the River Road and stayed consistently about a half mile from it. Following alongside the railroad track from St. Maryville to Morganza, it was a much straighter road than the River Road. They traveled with the river to their right and the tracks to their left. Just past Morganza, the other end of False River looped back to the Mississippi and nearly converged with it.

Isherwood took notes from the passenger seat of Old Blue. He had driven this road to his old job and back for two years, and had never noticed all the barns and orchards. *There's so much that we can use*, Isherwood thought. "Whoa," he called out suddenly to Patrick. "Look at that. Stop, stop."

Patrick put up a hand. "Hold on, bro. I can only stop this thing so fast. That trailer will keep on rolling right over us or jackknife or God knows what." He was still pretty inexperienced at pulling a trailer.

Isherwood couldn't wait for Patrick to park the rig before jumping out. "Wait until the car comes to a full and compl—ah heck, nevermind. I'm just talking to myself, aren't I." Patrick parked Old Blue in the middle of the highway and Justin settled in behind them.

"What gives?" Justin called out from the window of the Escalade. Patrick just shrugged as he jumped out of the vehicle to follow Isherwood.

Soon, they were both following Isherwood across the ditch in the general direction of the river. They realized what Isherwood had found nearly simultaneously.

"Can you believe they survived this close to the river?" Isherwood was asking them. He was standing on the first bar of a fence looking into a cattle pasture. It was a small enclosure and held just one animal.

"Dude, I ain't loading that sucker up by myself," Justin growled.

"Isherwood found us a bull!" Patrick said, following Isherwood onto the fence. "Wow. And not just any bull, a freakin' longhorn."

"Yeah, and there's more cattle over there, too." Isherwood said pointing. "We can at least load up some of them. Uh, I think."

Luckily, it was easy enough to load up a few of the cows. They seemed to be starving. The enclosure was likely too small for their numbers. The hard part was Patrick trying to back up the trailer into the pasture. He needed to learn how to handle the trailer himself, but the endless advice that Isherwood and Justin kept barking at him was doing more harm than good. Eventually, Justin took over.

They loaded up four cows, two side-by-side in the front two bays. This left the third bay at the back of the trailer empty and likely large enough to accommodate the longhorn.

"Are we really about to do this?" Justin asked, staring back at the bull in the first enclosure.

Isherwood raised his hands in a shrug. "I don't want to do it, either. Believe me. But when are we ever gonna get this lucky again? I mean, the day right after Monsignor asks us to start looking, we find breeding stock? Who knows? This could be the last one we see for months or ever."

"Alright," Justin said shaking his head. "Let's just do this before I lose my nerve." He hopped back into Old Blue and started moving the rig to the other side of the pasture where the gate to the bull enclosure stood. Patrick had decided to start patrolling around the pasture and his two buddies. There were few houses along the road to Morganza and they were widely spaced. He had his .22 slung over his shoulder, but he'd likely only need his knife. The report of the rifle would likely be the end of the remaining cattle, as the zombies would probably finally come to notice the walking meat. As yet, there was next to no zombie activity in the area, even with the river levees less than a few hundred yards away. This section of the river seemed straighter than the river bend they had fought near the other day. They were starting to think they understood how the River Dead phenomenon worked. Maybe.

Isherwood gathered up an armful of hay and took a shortcut to meet Justin at the gate. He had cut the shackle of the padlock with the bolt cutters and was ready to swing open the gate once Justin got in position. The trailer slid neatly through the open gate, leaving just enough room for Isherwood to pass through comfortably. He made sure the door to the inside of the trailer was unlocked and ajar before stepping into the trailer to lure the bull inside the last bay. The door was his escape route, but he was fully prepared to hop the partition and stand with the cows if the bull got friendly.

The bull, too, was surprisingly docile, despite the smell of Isherwood's fear being thick in the air. Isherwood clicked a few times and waved the fresh hay at the bull and he strode right up the ramp and into the last bay. Justin was right behind him lifting up the tailgate and latching it in place as Isherwood scooted out the trailer's side door.

"Phew," Isherwood exhaled audibly, as he leaned back against the trailer. "I thought zombies were scary. That thing is *way* bigger up close."

"I'm just glad we loaded the cattle two-by-two," Justin said. "Or else, that big'un would be lifting up the front half of the trailer and Old Blue with it."

"I feel like we should go back and drop these guys off, before pressing on to Morganza. But we're almost there."

"Isherwood," Justin said, scratching his head. "But dude, where're we gonna put these things. They can't just run free around the church. They'll tear right through all the plantings and likely gore holes through all the kids."

Isherwood had put his hands on his hips to think. "Well," he said finally. "There's always Monsignor's backyard. How about a bull staring you down while you drink your morning coffee? We'll just have to build some fences. Might as well press on to Morganza. We'll need more people to help us build all these fences. It'd be nice for us to expand our territory, maybe enclosing some extra homes for all the families. A second layer of fortifications would be great, too."

"Well, if we're gonna do all that," Justin said pausing. "We might as well try to get all the rest of the cattle, too. There's gotta be a truck and cattle trailer on this property right here, don't'ya think?"

Isherwood was laughing and shaking his head.

"What?" Justin said, mildly insulted.

"You mean like *that* one?" Isherwood was pointing farther up the driveway towards the house at the back of the property. "Looks like Ol' Patty has thought right past us."

Justin turned to see Patrick driving towards them in a silver truck pulling a cattle trailer. It was a dually Dodge Ram 3500 and clearly a diesel. The power windows were rolling down as Patrick pulled up. He yelled through the cab, "It's got a hemi!"

"Well, I guess so," Isherwood smiled. "I didn't know you knew how to hotwire!"

Patrick shrugged, "I don't. The keys were right under the visor. A shiny new apple just waiting to be picked."

In another hour or so, they had loaded up another eight cows. Patrick seemed to be having much better luck maneuvering this trailer than the one before. There were still another dozen or so, which they had to leave behind. These would likely be devoured by the zombies that all their noise would have inevitably drawn in. They were soon back on their way to Morganza, only another three miles or so down the road.

CHAPTER TWENTY-ONE: PADRE

The Three Amigos caravan once again included three vehicles. Isherwood had taken over driving Old Blue, as Patrick had taken a liking to the new Dodge. Despite the change in driver, Old Blue was again at the head of the column. It had now become tradition, even superstition.

Isherwood took mental note as they passed the Laurent Brothers service shop. This had always marked the beginning of Morganza in Isherwood's mind. It was also where he would cross the railroad tracks to go to Sara's grandmother's house, her father's mother. The woman was sort of the matriarch of the town, having given birth to a large share of its population, who in turn spawned an even larger share of the population. Sara's father, Glenn, had been one of thirteen children. Sadly, Sara's Mawmaw had died the year before. It now appeared like a special grace for her to have died before the world became so inhospitable.

They passed the old high school. It was a three-story brick building surrounded by a somewhat sturdy fence, Isherwood took note. After another half mile, they passed the old fueling station and the remains of Melancon's Café where the movie *Easy Rider* had been filmed years before. Next, Old Blue led the caravan across the railroad tracks down a short street which led directly to the front doors of St. Anne's church. A large field stood empty and green before the church. Isherwood had never really noticed the fence encircling the church before. Its cast iron bars looked nearly as sturdy and tall as St. Mary's.

But the very first thing they all noticed were the electric lights blinking on to welcome them. They parked the caravan in the middle of the road that crossed perpendicular in front of the church.

"Son of a gun got electricity!" Justin called out as the driver's side doors all clanked open along the church-side of the road.

"The son of a gun's got a bicycle generator," a voice called out. "And a gun, too, while we're on the topic."

"Dang, it's good to hear that voice. Come on out, Padre! It's me, Isherwood, and some friends. We've come as emissaries of the new Abbot Monsignor or Monsignor Abbot or whatever of St. Mary's. Civilization has returned to Morganza, more or less."

A tall, thickly-built man in a black cassock threw open the doors to the church and walked out with his arms lifted wide. He had black-rimmed glasses and a coarse black thicket growing across his face which poorly concealed a broad white smile. He looked like a mountain man stuffed into black priest's robes. Two small cats slinked out of the church after the big priest.

He strode to the front gate without saying anymore, but the wide smile remained etched across his face. As he drew near, they could see he was a younger man. Though Isherwood was actually the eldest, the four men were all about the same age.

"Come on in," Father Simeon beckoned. "I was wondering when you'd get here."

"Wait–" Patrick turned to the priest suspiciously. "You knew we were coming?"

"Mmm-huh," Simeon nodded.

"But how?"

"Little birdie told me," Simeon answered, smiling with an unreadable gaze. A moment later, Simeon returned to the group after latching the gate back. They just stood for a moment trying not to look at each other.

Simeon seemed far more at ease in the uncomfortable quiet than the others.

Justin finally broke the silence, "So, what's the plan, eh? Does that fence run all the way around to the back of the cemetery?"

"It does," Simeon nodded. "I see you've brought a herd along with you."

"And some bales of hay," Isherwood added. "You saying we could use your church grounds to give them a home? This would be perfect, Padre. *Perfect.*"

Padre just nodded in answer, rocking back and forth a bit with his hands pushed down into the deep pockets of his cassock.

Isherwood was smiling slyly. "Bicycle generator, you say? You know, Padre. The only thing that could make this *more* perfect is if that generator of yours meant we could all share a round of cold beers."

Padre slowly raised his still-smiling bearded face. "Indeed," he said leading them over to the Rectory. "I think I still owe *you* a few, Isherwood, don't I?"

"Maybe, but one cold, post-apocalypse beer would be worth an infinity of pre-apocalypse beers," Isherwood answered.

*****

"I guess I ought to have asked this sooner," Isherwood said, after he had taken his time consuming possibly one of the last cold beers left on earth. They were all sitting around the oak kitchen table of the rectory. The cats took turns preening themselves around the men's boots. "Excuse me," he said belching. "Is it just you here? Any others?"

"Oh yeah," Padre answered. "There's a few around. There used to be more, but –" He stopped there, not feeling the need to say anymore.

Patrick wrinkled his nose. "Uh, where are they?"

"They're not here, of course. They come and go."

"Man," Justin said. "They the loner type or something?" Father just shrugged in answer.

"Do they live nearby or out in the woods?"

"There's two that live in town. One lives somewhere out in the middle of the spillway. Call him Carrot."

"Carrot?" Isherwood laughed. "Is he red-headed or something?"

"Nah," Padre said. "He just sort of pops up here and there. Should really be called gopher, but so it goes."

"You think they'd be willing to join up with us? Or, are they the unsavory sort?"

Padre leaned back in his chair to consider the question for a time. "Maybe, but they don't seem to have much cause to just now."

"Y'all haven't had any zombies coming up out of the river?" Isherwood asked incredulously.

Padre leaned forward and put down his beer. "Come again?"

"Padre," Patrick said. "We had basically emptied the town of zombies, and then we went scouting along the levees. We put down, after nearly a whole afternoon, about a thousand."

Padre looked to the other faces for confirmation. Isherwood was nodding, "The river must've carried them from wherever. It just sort of belches them up, we think. Padre," he said emphatically. "They don't drown."

"They just get soggy," Justin added.

Padre nodded. "You know, I think we ought to round those guys up." Even as he said it, there came a sound of iron bars rattling. They left their beers and hurried out of the rectory back to the gates. There were two men and a woman at the gate. They weren't looking through the gate to the church, but backward. It was then that they noticed the moans coming up from the spillway. The sound drifted their way on the wind. It was a low sound composed of many thousand voices.

"Looks like the zombies already rounded them up for us," Justin said as Padre was busy opening the gate. "That's the good news."

"The—they—they're," the woman was saying breathlessly. "They're coming up the spillway."

"Guys, this is Agnes, her husband Jim, and Marshall." Padre introduced the two groups. They were each carrying either a pistol or a rifle. They each also had knives and some other kind of bludgeoning weapon.

"Alright," Patrick said. "Where should we draw the line?"

"What's that?" Padre asked calmly. The priest seemed to be growing calmer the crazier things became. Isherwood explained how they marked out a range and allowed the zombies to walk into the kill zone and slowly build up a barricade with their corpses. Isherwood suggested that they mark out their range in the open field at the front of the church.

"Yeah, nice clear line of sight, but we'll need to guide them in somehow," Justin suggested.

"He's right," Marshall was nodding. "We'll have to lead them up along the highway, and then make them take a sharp turn."

"Looks like they're already doing half our job for us," Padre nodded back toward the Morganza Highway the men had driven in on. Everybody turned. The leading edge of the horde was trickling in along the road. They hadn't yet noticed their group in the churchyard.

"Come on, guys," Isherwood said in a hush. "Let's get our trucks inside the gate. We can start firing from there, if the sound of the trucks doesn't bring them in our guns will."

Patrick was on the radio as he ran to his new Dodge truck. He was updating St. Mary's of their situation. "We've found survivors at St. Anne's, Padre among them, but a horde of RDs arrived just after us. We're fine here. This church has strong fences, too."

Old Blue led the three vehicles into the elliptical driveway in front of the church. They followed the driveway around and then turned sharply onto the grass so that the trucks were parallel to the fence. They parked as close to the fences as possible to provide counter pressure to the fences in case the zombies overwhelmed the barricades.

"We've got one extra .22 and about two thousand rounds between us," Isherwood was explaining. "Jim, what kind of rifle you got? Is that a .22?"

"Nah, it's a .270," he explained.

"That's fine," Isherwood was nodding. "I think we've got about a hundred rounds for a .270 and an extra one in Old Blue when yours overheats. Maybe you and your wife could lay down on top of that cattle trailer right there – the one without the bull in it. We've got a turret in the Escalade and the bed of Old Blue, too. Hey, where's Padre?"

"I'm right here," he called out. They looked around, but didn't see the priest. "Up here," he called out. They looked up, following the priest's voice all the way up to the church's west bell tower. Two towers rose from either side of the church's front façade. Padre was laid out in the one closest to them, looking through the scope of a high-powered rifle. "I've got three more rifles up here, and – BLAM, *ckshhh*!" He paused blowing the head off the first zombie to cross their imaginary line of demarcation about seventy-five yards in front of the church fence. "— and about three hundred rounds. The rest of the Morganza police department's armory is in the front bedroom of the rectory. Help yourselves."

"Hey, Padre!" Isherwood called up to the bell tower. "Will you help us watch out for zeds coming from over there?" He was pointing down along the road that ran east-west in front of the church. There was another side street connecting the Morganza Highway to the church road. The zombies could easily start coming from that side, which would make for a bad shooting angle. They would also need to divert some of their people to cover the new direction. So far, there were only one or two trickling in down the church road.

Padre nodded. "Once they get past the Rectory, though, my line of sight gets blocked."

"Hey, Padre," Justin called up. "How about a quick blessing? This horde's looking pretty ugly." They looked back to see Padre raising his arm and marking a cross in the air.

The new survivors took pretty quickly to the new strategy. They were forming a neat line at about 75 yards. The zombies were still trying to stumble and crawl over the mound. They would continue to do this, Isherwood had observed, until the mound reached about chest level and began to obscure the zombie's peripheral vision. Either the zombies were just focused in on their prey and had tunnel vision, or else their visual field had contracted somewhat. Zombies don't blink, Isherwood knew. The lenses of their eyes were gradually obscured and grayed by a thousand little scratches.

Once the mound grew high enough, they would begin staggering around the outer wings of it. The shooters used this movement to lengthen the mounds until they expanded enough to run into some manmade obstacle, usually the side of a house or building. The expanding mounds would gradually curve inward since the shooting line was relatively short, only ever ten or twenty feet long. Eventually, if there were no obstacles, the mound would encircle the shooters. There would come a time, Isherwood mused, that they may have to fight on open ground and not behind a fence. If that happened, they could use this strategy to build a wall around their position. If there were just a few shooters, they would need to shoot back-to-back. They would literally be circling the wagons. Once the mounds grew high enough, they would just need to shoot the heads of the zombies as they came crawling over the top. When it was time to get out of the zombie atoll, though, they would have to be very careful climbing over the mounds. There would likely be a number of zombies that were still squirming inside the mounds, who had become trapped inside during a z-landslide or avalanche.

After an hour of constant shooting and re-loading, the z-mound at seventy-five yards was about twenty yards wide and four feet high. It was already starting to grow longer. Padre had made another mound about three-feet high across the road running east-west in front of the church. Between the two slowly expanding walls was a house surrounded by a short chain-link fence.

Isherwood was resting a moment, but still watching the kill zone in front of the church. It was about three in the afternoon. He was reloading his spare .22, and making sure the others were also good for ammo. "Hey, Padre," he called up to the bell tower. "What's it looking like upstream?"

"What's that?" Father Simeon said lifting his head from his rifle and waiting a moment for the ringing in his ears to subside.

"Upstream? You know, up-horde? Any signs of slowing down? Any leaks opening up around the kill zone?"

"I can't see down the highway," Padre was shaking his head. "Pretty steady up and over the railroad tracks. As the wind changed a little while ago, it sounded like the moans were still coming from pretty far out."

Isherwood nodded, sighing, "If they're still coming by the time it gets dark, we'll put our headlights on 'em. We could always start mounding again at thirty or so yards for those that make it over the top."

"How's the ammo situation?" Padre asked.

"We've probably got through three or four hundred rounds so far. We're about a quarter to a third out. And that's not counting whatever you've got stashed in the Rectory."

Padre nodded in agreement and fell quiet. He soon put his head back to the scope of his rifle. Isherwood walked off awkwardly and went about passing out bottles of water to the new guys. The two men and the woman were on the right side of the firing line. He encouraged them to watch out for the zombies that would soon start coming in greater numbers around their side of the mound. He subbed in for them as they gulped down some water hastily. It was a cool, Spring day, but the heat from the rifles accumulated quickly.

After another hour, the zombies were crashing through the yard between the larger mound and Padre's side mound. The zombies started spilling through the windows of the small house between the mounds. Isherwood called out for Padre and Justin, who were all working the left half of the kill zone now, to help him plug the windows with the corpses. Next, they dropped the zombies as they came up against the short chain link fence. The space between the house and the fence quickly clogged up with zombies and the mounds collided with each other.

By 5:00pm, the St. Mary's ammo supplies began running dangerously low. By this time, however, the mounds were rising past twelve feet or up to the roofline of the Rectory. The long semi-circular mound had terminated in a line of houses on the right side of the kill zone, or back towards St. Maryville. This was fortunate because it left one side of the road in front of the church open to the trucks as an escape route. The left side was petering out about thirty degrees past the ditch that ran along the road in front of the church. The zombies were now mostly coming straight on, trying to climb up the slippery outer slope of the mound. Their heads kept popping over the crest of the mound.

Patrick was getting really good at picking off the heads as they popped up. He called them "gophers" – "You know," he explained, "like on the old Nintendo duck hunt? That little gopher would pop up in the foreground after the end of a round of shooting the ducks. You don't remember that little guy? He'd be holding all the dead ducks?"

"You're losing it, man," Justin smirked. "That was a *dog*. You know, a *bird* dog?"

"Oh, right. You're right," Patrick nodded, remembering. A couple seconds later, he was back to calling them gophers. Justin cursed, but started his little screeching laugh when he noticed Isherwood shaking his head at both of them.

Around 6:00pm, they finally started taking ammo from Padre's cache in the Rectory. "Go ahead," Padre encouraged them. "Take some. Just help me gather up all the spent casings when we're done here – and I think we are about to be done here."

"You don't want us to litter, Father?" Marshall asked.

"Not exactly, but that's good, too," Padre answered mysteriously.

Isherwood was smiling broadly. "Padre! What've you got up your sleeve? You got yourself a bullet factory, don't you?" Padre didn't answer, but he was nodding and grinning.

"No way!" Justin said, looking shocked. "You stinkin' idiot. That's amazing. You got lead and everything?"

Padre nodded, "Yup, and about forty pounds of gunpowder."

Justin's jaw loosened a bit at that. He turned his head, mumbling to himself. "Forty pounds? But that would be – well, for a .22LR – that would be like two, no three thousand or so bullets per *pound*. That's like enough powder for over, uh, over a hundred thousand bullets!"

Padre had pushed out his bottom lip a bit and was nodding. "Got a nice little furnace, too, but I'll need some help pedaling the bicycle generator for that."

All Justin could manage to say was, "Dude."

After another hour or so, around night fall, they began taking shifts shooting the "gopher" heads that were still popping up over the crest of the long mound. It had grown another couple feet in height at the crest. Not only were fewer and fewer people needed, but they wanted to start muffling the sound of the rifles and they only had two suppressors that would fit the rifles. They decided to bed down for the night after Padre made them a light, but hot meal. They divided up the night into shifts. By the fourth watch of the night, they had shut off all the trucks and were only using knives and flashlights to kill the ones that had managed to climb over the mound and stagger into the fence.

CHAPTER TWENTY-TWO:
COWS AND CODDLING

They awoke early the next morning before dawn. Marshall had had the last shift. There were just a couple zombies still groping through the cast iron bars of the church's tall fence. These were easily and soundlessly dispatched with knives. Now that they had killed so many, they hoped to move out without attracting the notice of another wave.

Before heading back to St. Maryville, they first unloaded the cattle. They started with the trailer without the bull. Father Simeon would allow the cattle to roam freely across the property. They would be protected inside the fences. There was plenty of grass for now, too, but they would probably still need to bring in some bales of hay. They unloaded the eight cows from the second trailer, but the bull prevented them from unloading the first trailer.

Father had an idea for what to do with the bull. The church's fence ran all around the church property, including the large cemetery at the back of the church. The older section of the cemetery was further enclosed with another heavy cast iron fence. It was filled with ornate vaults and statues. It appeared from a distance like the downtown section of a miniature city with the vaults rising tall like skyscrapers. Altogether, the smaller cemetery within a cemetery enclosed almost an acre. There was plenty of tall green grass between the rows of vaults, as well.

"Whoa," Justin said, overhearing a conversation between Father Simeon and Isherwood. "Padre's coming back with us?" They had all just finished unloading the bull into the older section of the cemetery. Jim, Agne's husband, had taken over driving the truck and trailer. He seemed to have quite a bit of skill behind the wheel.

Isherwood and the priest interrupted their private conversation and turned to Justin. Isherwood nodded, "Yeah, that's right, but we don't want to leave the church completely unattended, even temporarily."

The others were drawing closer, as well. "We've been talking, Father." It was Agnes with her husband, Jim. "We wouldn't mind staying and taking care of the animals."

"You two wouldn't mind?" Isherwood asked. "This place could get swarmed again, even with the walls of corpses as barricades. And my stomach's already starting to turn at the smell."

Agnes looked back to her husband and exchanged nods. "Just so long," Jim insisted, "as you provide us with a good bit of ammo and maybe one of the vehicles, in case we need to bug out your way."

Isherwood nodded heavily in answer. Padre added, "Of course! Matter of fact, I would've insisted on it. You two have experience with cattle?"

"Yes, Father. Quite a bit, actually. Jim's managed pasture land on the side for years." Agnes answered. Jim hitched a thumb in one of his belt loops, apparently feeling abashed all of a sudden.

"Is that right, Mr. Jim?" Father Simeon nodded in admiration.

"Yes, Father," Jim answered, looking at the priest from the corner of his eye.

"Don't mind him, Father," Agnes said confidentially. "It's just we've always wanted our own piece of land, you see? Jim's always wanted a herd of his own. With your say-so, you're sorta answering prayers we've had for, well, for quite a long time."

164

"It's done then," Padre said. "You're really helping a lot of people, Jim and Agnes. I hope you know that and this, as well – it's no mere coincidence that you're here and alive, or that any of us are still here, for that matter. We have just enough gifts and talents between us to begin turning things around. But *only* enough."

"We'll take good care of 'em, Father. Just you wait and see. You'll be real proud of this herd."

They left Jim and Agnes a short while later, leaving out the front gate and passing through the still-unblocked half of the church road. Before leaving, Father Simeon had taken Jim and Agnes aside and walked them through the process for manufacturing bullets. He also left them with an instructional book and all the used brass casings from the night before. There were a few more books on the subject, Father explained, in the small library branch along the highway. Jim already had some experience with the manufacturing process, and they were both already familiar with Padre's preparations for the apocalypse, including the bicycle generator.

The caravan again had Old Blue at the head and the Escalade following behind. As they crested over the railroad tracks, they were happy to see that the Morganza highway was just an empty stretch of highway again. It showed no sign of the previous day's grisly parade. The open road looked inviting enough, again appearing as it likely once had to the crew of *Easy Rider*. They had weathered the storm, for now.

*****

They were relieved to find the church grounds in a much more tranquil state than the last time they had returned home from a bruising shoot-out. The air, however, was thick with the smell of rotting flesh. The moaning of the zombies had been replaced by a low buzzing sound. Clouds of flies were darkening the sky farther down Main Street, where they had left the mounds to rot. Isherwood shivered in disgust at the thought of the mounds of flesh being replaced by mountains of squirming maggots. His thoughts turned to how they could set fire to the mounds before disease began spreading to their doorstep and also how they could avoid burning down the whole town in the process.

These thoughts quickly evaporated as Sara came running toward the caravan as they were opening the back gate. Her face was stricken and she was crying. All the men poured out of the trucks at the sight of her. She just buried her face in Isherwood's chest for a time, as she tried catching her breath long enough to tell him what had happened.

Isherwood was mentally preparing himself for the worst. "Where are the children, Sara? Where are Emma Claire and Charlie?"

Sara wasn't able to regain her composure for some time, but the sound of the truck engines and the gate opening had drawn the others to them. Gran explained that Emma had been taken. "Not by zombies," she said. "We saw a car driving away right after we noticed that Emma had disappeared."

"What can you tell us about the car?" Father Simeon asked. "Did it have any markings? Could you hear how far it went and in which direction?"

"It was headed back towards Hospital Road," Tad answered. "It was dirty, but I think it was a brown sedan. Somebody had drawn something in the dust on the back windshield."

"What?" Isherwood said with madness barely veiled in his voice. "What was drawn, Tad?"

"Three crosses," She said without looking Isherwood in the eye.

"Three crosses? Hospital Road?" Isherwood said in astonishment.

Justin was shaking his head. "What? What does that mean? You know where they took her from *that*?" Isherwood didn't answer him. He had stormed off and was busy digging through the back of Old Blue.

"Patrick," he said, coming back holding the automatic rifles. "How much ammo do you still have for these?"

"Enough," Patrick answered gravely. "Enough."

"Hello! Would somebody answer me?" Justin was calling out. "What aren't you people saying?"

"It's Tad's and Jerry's wacko church," Isherwood called out from the trunk area of the Escalade. "It's that converted roller rink or bowling alley or wherever those rapture freaks set up shop. They've got three crosses out front, and they're gonna hang from them if they've hurt her. Where's your rope, Patrick? I put rope in every one of these —"

"It's right here, buddy," Patrick said, showing Isherwood the rope that was laying right in the center of the truck bed. He exchanged glances with Justin and Father Simeon.

Padre nodded. "Alright, Isherwood. Let's load back up. We're coming with you and we'll go right now, but listen, buddy."

"I don't need help," Isherwood said rummaging violently in the back of Old Blue. "But *they* will."

Padre nodded to Patrick, who nodded back. "Look, man," Patrick started saying as he walked straight up to Isherwood. "We can't do this if you're gonna go over there all half-cocked and stupid, okay?"

Isherwood rounded on his friend. His eyes were enflamed with malice. He was about to charge Patrick while gripping his rifle with white knuckles, when Father Simeon appeared behind him. The priest brought down the butt of a pistol hard onto the back of Isherwood's skull. Isherwood collapsed under the impact. Padre snatched the rifle from Isherwood's clutch just before he fell on top of it. "Get him in the truck," the priest called to Justin and Patrick. "He'll be up and ready by the time we get to Hospital Road."

"We never went down Hospital Road," Patrick was saying, as he lifted Isherwood's unconscious body by the feet. Justin was carrying his head and shoulders. They tossed him as gingerly as possible into the cab of Old Blue. Sara went over to him, still trying to choke down her sobs.

Patrick was still thinking aloud. "We'd avoided it all this time because it was swarming with zombies. This little rat's nest has been waiting there all this time. We probably even helped these nutbags along by drawing the swarm away. If we'd done nothing, they'd have probably already starved to death in their building surrounded by the dead."

"I'm sure we'll make it right soon enough," Justin said grimly.

Gran and the rest were still standing by watching the men prepare to leave. "Do you need Tad to come with you?" Gran asked. "Shouldn't you at least ask her what this place looks like on the inside – is there a back door? Maybe a way in through the roof?"

Justin and Patrick turned to the older woman, clearly impressed. Tad looked back at Gran almost offended, but Gran pressed on. "What? You don't think you're partly responsible? You've been associating with these fools for the last thirty years, dear. Coddling madness, *hmmph*. You think you can just make up a religion from whole cloth without consequences?"

Justin whistled in appreciation. "Better do what she says, Ms. Tad."

CHAPTER TWENTY-THREE: COJONES

In the end and over the fierce protests of Jerry, Tad agreed to accompany Father Simeon and the other men to the church with the three crosses. They had left Marshall at St. Mary's to help guard, along with Jerry, against any further attacks from the mysterious group.

As Gran had anticipated, there was both a back door and roof access to the converted bowling alley. Tad advised against coming in through the front. They would be wide open if they entered down the church's long driveway. They would also have to take Hospital Road head on. They decided to come from the back, even though this meant driving through the same sugar cane fields that stood at the back of Wal-Mart. Father Simeon thought they could probably find some rougher roads leading to the back of the cane fields. Driving straight across the furrowed cane field would likely make a lot of racket.

They decided to approach quietly and observe the compound first from behind the cover of adjacent buildings. Tad had also seen the dirty brown sedan driving away. They hoped she would be able to identify it, if they ran across it in the bowling alley parking lot or elsewhere.

They were all standing in a fenced in backyard in Major Subdivision when Isherwood awoke from his nap. It had been Justin's backyard until recently. They had avoided Major Parkway to get there, driving instead through another adjacent subdivision east of there. There was a direct line of sight past the Civic Center and across the cane fields to the back of the old bowling alley. They were looking through their binoculars.

"We need a telescope to see anything at this distance," Patrick said. Even still, they could see a sizeable ring of zombies surrounding the back of the bowling alley. They could also see, though obscured by a stand of sugar cane, the dust-covered sedan that had led them there in the first place.

Justin shook his head, "Yeah, but wind is coming from the west. We're in a good spot to listen. Besides, didn't the Aycock kid have a telescope?" Justin and Patrick had both lived in this subdivision until Isherwood had driven by over a week ago, leading the dead behind him like the pied piper.

"Yeah, I think you're right," Patrick agreed.

"Let's go get it, then. We should have a good view from your second floor deck."

"Knives only, guys," Padre reminded them. They were leaving just as the truck door was slowly creaking open. Isherwood was sitting just inside, rubbing his head. Justin saluted him in passing.

Patrick hushed him quickly, as Isherwood, suddenly aware of his surroundings, made to start yelling again. "Go talk to Padre. He'll explain," Patrick said in hushed tones.

Isherwood staggered over to Padre who was still watching over the top of the fence. Staggering, he resembled a zombie, himself. He was rubbing his eyes, trying to make them focus. "Hidey-ho, Wilson," he said groggily with a weak smile.

"Did you just make a *Home Improvement* joke?" Padre asked, shaking his head in disdain. "Wouldn't we need to be on opposite sides of the fence for that?"

Isherwood sneered back at the priest. "What? So you could sucker punch me again?"

170

The priest was shaking his head. "That wasn't a sucker punch, that was cold-cocking."

"Whatever, jerk," Isherwood said, but his smile had started growing stronger. It then arched into a sneer as the image of his daughter flashed across his mind.

"You know as well as Padre that you needed a good blow to the head," Tad said from the tailgate of the truck. She was sitting there hanging her feet over the side. She was barefooted, as always.

Isherwood whirled around. "What're *you* doing here?" There was a thick note of blame in his voice. At the sight of her, the madness was again beginning to stir in his eyes.

"These are *my* people, remember?" Tad said. "Did Padre knock you out before or after your Gran's little indictment?"

Isherwood went over to Old Blue to lean against its side as he spoke to Tad. "*Your* people, right. Guess I'm not the only one that needed a good blow to the head."

Tad didn't respond immediately, but allowed for a long pause. Isherwood looked at her strangely, and noticed for the first time that she was smoking a cigarette. He couldn't decide what was weirder. He'd never seen her smoke, and she never paused before responding to his jabs at her religion.

"You alright, Aunt Tad?" he asked again. The edge had fallen from his tone.

She gave him a sidelong glance and then returned to her cigarette. He saw that her eyes were ringed in red. "I will be," she said. Subconsciously, Isherwood retreated backwards with his head and shoulders as though edging away from a snake.

"So, what's the play?" Isherwood asked Padre, after putting some space between himself and Tad, though never taking his eyes off of her.

Father Simeon shrugged. "Not much we can do. We have no way of knowing they'll ever come out of there again. They probably have enough of a stockpile in there, so they don't need to leave anytime soon. Can't really smoke them out, or your daughter might be forced into that ring of zombies around the building. Don't take this the wrong way, but they might be preparing to drink the Kool-Aid."

"So, what then?" Isherwood asked. "Go in guns blazing?"

Father Simeon just nodded, dolefully.

"Lock and load."

*****

Isherwood grew increasingly anxious, as they waited for Justin and Patrick to return with the telescope. When the two finally did return, they took turns looking through the telescope and decided that they knew no more now than they had without the telescope.

"Crap, guys!" Isherwood said, finally overwhelmed with waiting. "My little girl's less than a half mile from here. What the hell are we waiting for?"

"Where'd she go?" Padre said suddenly.

"What?" Isherwood growled. He clenched his fists, imagining himself ripping the Roman collar from Father Simeon's cassock as he threw him over the fence. "She's in that freakin' bowling alley church."

"No," Padre shook his head calmly. "Where is *Tad?*"

Isherwood felt as though the priest had thrown cold water in his face. He even moved to wipe the imaginary water from his chin.

"Dude," Justin said. "He's right. Where is she?"

"Did she have a gun?" Padre was asking. "Any missing from the truck, Patrick?"

"No," Isherwood answered.

"And no," Patrick followed up.

"Let me see that telescope," Isherwood barked, finally catching up to Padre's thinking. He jumped into the bed of the truck and yanked the aperture to his eye. They had set up the telescope in the bed of Old Blue instead of bringing it up onto the Fontenot's balcony. They had decided it would be too high profile.

172

"*Bi*—scuits and cheese," Isherwood cursed after wagging the telescope back and forth a couple times. Father Simeon and the others were standing along the fence looking through binoculars.

"How the –? She's nearly through the cane field," Patrick asked no one in particular.

"My God and she's unarmed," Simeon said, shaking his head.

"She's dead," Justin said.

"Nah, not yet," Isherwood said. His eyes were still twitching with madness. "But, come on. Get in the truck. We can still try chasing her down."

"Chasing her down?" Justin asked. "Are you nuts? We'll just draw those things away from the weirdo church and toward her."

Father Simeon shook his head. "No, we won't." He was following Isherwood hurriedly into the truck.

"Has everybody lost their minds?" Justin was calling out.

Patrick pushed him forward, trying to fish the truck keys out of his pocket. "Nah, man. Get in the truck. Don't you get it? If we go crazy trying to chase her down, it'll look like she's running from us." He quickly pulled his hands out of his pockets when he realized he had purposefully left the keys in the ignition for a quick getaway.

"She will be!" Justin marveled at his friends.

"She's banking on it!" Isherwood said, getting out to help pull Justin in the truck. "She knows we'd never have agreed otherwise."

Justin relaxed and let himself be dragged into Old Blue. "Can someone please explain all this to me?" he said from the backseat of Old Blue. "And what about the Escalade?"

Isherwood, sitting at shotgun, turned around to look at his two friends, while Father Simeon turned the key and cranked the truck into drive. "She's trying to make it look like she's running to them – to her old wacko friends – for sanctuary from *us*."

Recognition dawned across Justin's face. "From the crazy Catholics!"

"Right, it's brilliant," Patrick said. "They'll swallow that bait – hook, line, sinker, and pole. Like always."

Isherwood was nodding. "But she needs *us* to make enough crazy noise to, first, make it look like the crazy Catholics are trying to run her down rather than let her defect, and, second, to draw those zombies away from the back door and to us instead of her."

Justin was looking out the back windshield in admiration. "Man, that lady's got cojones."

"Though she be but little, she is fierce," Patrick echoed.

CHAPTER TWENTY-FOUR: BOWLING ALLEY CHURCHES

As they watched slack-jawed from inside Old Blue, Tad's plan – or so they assumed it to be – worked flawlessly. The zombies were spilling over themselves to chase after the honking truck as it bounced up and down, up and down driving madly through the cane field. Distracted, only one or two of them turned to see Tad banging on the back door of the bowling alley. Tad took care of these easily enough, stabbing a knife into their skulls between pounding on the metal industrial door.

It was the zombies that began streaming around the sides of the building that were the problem. Tad's act quickly became real as the zombies started closing in from each side. "Let me in! It's Tad – they're coming for me!"

She paused a moment. She dispatched another pair of zombies with her knife, but groups of five or more were within just feet of her. Just when the prickling sense of impending danger was about to snatch her backwards into full-scale retreat, the door opened. She was pulled inside just as the enclosing groups of zombies collided together smearing blood and rot against the closed door.

"Whoa!" Justin cooed from the backseat of Old Blue, letting out a deep sigh. "I thought she was dead on arrival. That chick's got some serious survival instincts."

"Yeah, glad she's safe and all, but we've got problems of our own," Padre said as the group of zombies peeled away from the bowling alley's back door to join the rest of the growing horde that was now throwing themselves headlong towards Old Blue. "What d'we do?" he asked. He was still driving the truck straight toward the back of the building and, now, straight into the oncoming zombies.

"Uh, just stop and growl a bit," Isherwood said. "You know, gun the engine or something. Make it sound disappointed and frustrated."

"How am I supposed to make the engine sound like that?" Padre asked shaking his head.

"I don't know – 'fly casual'," Isherwood sneered.

"What?" Padre roared, finally losing his cool.

"It's a *Star Wars* quote, Father," Patrick said.

"I –!" Father Simeon slammed his fist down on the steering wheel, arresting its motion just shy of impact. "I *know* it's a Star Wars quote. I know how to read a *schematic!*" Padre's momentary mood swing was forgotten. He began gunning the engine and honking.

"*That* was a *Jurassic Park* quote," Justin told Patrick.

They decided to let the zombies swarm the truck and then retreat backward across the cane field at the last possible moment. Once they were clear of the zombies and back on the smooth asphalt of Major Parkway, Padre pealed out loudly and pretended to tuck tail and run. Instead, they looped back around. They turned back on to Main Street and came back around through the back of the next subdivision. They re-entered the cane field from the opposite direction and under cover. There was, as they had suspected, an overgrown farm road running along the sides of the cane field. They followed this around to the back of the cane field, approaching the bowling alley again from the north side.

They tucked Old Blue under the drooping limbs of an overgrown willow tree. Isherwood, Padre, and Justin left Patrick behind to hide in the truck and be ready by the radio in case a quick getaway was needed.

The three men armed themselves with automatic rifles and pistols from the truck. They then climbed up a small embankment at the back of the cane field and took cover behind a brick shell of a building. It had been gutted long before the infected started showing up. They checked in quickly, but there were no signs of the church having posted a look-out there. They covered the open ground between the gutted-out building and the building that was closest to the bowling alley. This next building used to be a combination of restaurant, specialty meats store, and deer processing facility. They hid, crouching behind what used to be the place's smokehouse.

"Justin," Isherwood whispered. "Can you get up on top of this little building to see if they've got people on their roof?"

"Dude," Justin said, shaking his head. "This little shed will buckle right under me. 'Sides, they ain't got nobody up there. They would've started shooting at us when we were driving right at 'em. I don't think these people were planning long term, buddy, no offense."

Isherwood's whole body lurched with the thought. He was keeping the mad rush of fatherly instincts and insanity bottled up inside of him, but only just barely. "Well, what'd we do? Just sit here?"

"Yup," Padre nodded. "The place is brick and steel and, from what I can see, has no windows. Not a bad place to hole up. Gross for a church, though."

*****

So they waited. The zombies gradually re-formed their ring around the building, though the men couldn't understand why. They couldn't hear anything drawing the dead back to the spot. Nevertheless, the zombies again started beating on the brick and metal walls. Their horrible moaning drew others in, as well. Every once in a while, as a full hour passed by, a zombie would wander near their position behind the smokehouse. They came in already moaning, so they could dispatch them with their knives without caring about making more noise.

Isherwood's resolve finally broke after an hour. Flashes of what those freaks might be doing to his daughter finally drove him to the brink. He cursed himself for ever reading *The Shack*. He raised himself from the back of the smokehouse and strode out from behind it before the other two could stop him. He was going to blow off the sides of this building and nothing was going to stop him. He clicked his rifle to full automatic and began mowing down the layers of zombies banging against the bowling alley's walls.

Just as he did, the back door rattled ajar and closed again under the weight of zombies pressing in. Isherwood flanked to his left and began drawing the zombies towards him and away from the door. As soon as they had advanced a couple feet, he mowed down a clean stripe of ten or twelve. The door opened again. Its ragged bottom scraped along a concrete sidewalk. It was Tad and she was holding Emma Claire on her hip. There was a small doorstop attached to the inside bottom of the door. Tad stomped on it with a bare foot, wedging the door wide open. Isherwood could hear music coming from within. Half of the zombies began pouring through the open door. The others lunged after the woman and the child. These met with the full wrath of the deranged father.

Father Simeon had to run after Isherwood and pull him back, or he would have spilled into the church along with the zombies and likely for the same purpose.

"You just left the door open?" Justin asked Tad as he ran up to her and Emma Claire. They could hear Patrick already gunning Old Blue's engine behind them. "There wasn't anybody we could save in there?"

The older woman turned to him with a withering stare. "Let the dead bury their dead."

CHAPTER TWENTY-FIVE: RADIO

Before they had turned back down Main Street, Padre asked that Patrick drive them through the front of the Wal-Mart parking lot. There, they would be able to see if anybody or anything was coming out the front of the church. Even if the occupants of the bowling alley had spilled out the front entrance to escape the zombies spilling in the back door, there were more zombies waiting out front to devour them.

In the end, they saw no one leave the church. "Guess they were waiting on the zombies to rapture them away," Justin remarked darkly. They would later find out that Justin's quip had been eerily spot-on.

Tad was quiet on the way home. She and Emma Claire had been the only ones to see inside the church, and neither one seemed to want to talk about the experience.

Emma Claire, they were all relieved to see, wanted nothing more than to snuggle up in the back seat with Isherwood. She was sucking her thumb hard, but even this was not completely out of the normal. Her dress, they saw, was still clean. No rips, no blood. It seemed they had retrieved the little girl before any permanent damage had been done by her kidnappers. Padre was especially relieved to see her wanting to be close to her dad, but he knew there just hadn't been time for Stockholm Syndrome or anything like that to have set in.

*****

Sara was still waiting at the church's back gate when Old Blue turned the corner. Marshall, too, came running when he saw the truck return. Sara fell to her knees hugging Emma Claire when the little girl came jumping out of the truck's back door. "Ma-mommy, ma-mommy," she said. "Those people smelled bad."

Isherwood eased himself out of the truck, feeling like he was just coming back from a bender. He hobbled over to where his wife and daughter were kneeling and just slid down until his head rested on Sara or Emma Claire, he didn't know which.

Gran eventually succeeded in bringing her grandson and his family back into the Rectory. She had a pot of coffee waiting for them that she had French-dripped on the gas stove. Monsignor greeted Father Simeon warmly. Father Simeon was bringing the older priest up to speed on his own church and what had happened the last couple days, when Tad interrupted them. She whispered something into Monsignor's ear, and he led her out the side door of Rectory.

Soon, they were all sitting around the dining room table beginning to unwind slowly. The wives informed their husbands of the progress made on the gardens and that only small groups of "Zacks" – that's what the ladies had taken to calling them to avoid scaring the children – had been coming to the fences. The men just let the women talk, being too tired to do anything but listen. Padre was better at listening, anyway.

Denise, Patrick's wife, went back over how Emma Claire had been playing with her boy, Huck, before she disappeared. They just couldn't understand how it had happened so quickly – how they hadn't even seen the car drive up. So much of it still didn't make sense to them.

Chelsea tried prying information from her husband, Justin, but he was starting to fall asleep on her shoulder.

Isherwood, too, was beginning to nod off. Sara kept pushing him backwards as his head kept sliding slowly and inexorably down into his ceramic mug of coffee.

"I must not have put enough juice in this coffee," Gran said, looking comically down into her old coffee mug. She soon joined in the laughter as Sara and the rest busted out laughing.

Just then, Vanessa came hurriedly into the Rectory. The ladies had forgotten about her in all the excitement of the men returning home with Emma Claire. "Oh, Vanessa," Gran said. "They're back – can you believe it? It looks like nobody was –"

"Yes, ma'am," Vanessa interrupted. At the sound of her voice, the men suddenly grew alert again. "That's amaz– I can't believe how luck– but listen," she said interrupting herself. "Sara." At the sound of her name, Sara put her hand to her chest. She had already had a long enough emotional rollercoaster that day. "I've made *contact*."

"You've got to be kidding me," Isherwood said. His head and shoulders fell in dismay. "With who? With Whiskey Bay? Oh, please, tell me it's good news."

"It's gotta be pretty good, right?" Sara was saying, growing breathless with excitement. Without knowing it, she had stood up beside the table. "They're alive if they're using the radio, right? Right?"

Vanessa was waving her hands for them to stop talking. "Let the girl speak," Gran insisted.

"They're under siege," she said, relaxing a bit after finally getting the words out. "I-10 was just—there were just so many, spilling over the elevated roadway into the swamp and coming down the exit ramps. Even after evacuating from the mainland to the island or whatever, they're still surrounded. Their camp is raised up on piers and they've destroyed the stairs but they're pinned in. There's just no way – they say the camp is surrounded by thousands of 'em."

"Did they say how long they've got until their supplies run out?" Isherwood asked.

"Yesterday," Vanessa said sighing. "If it rains, they'll be able to replenish their water. But they've already started fasting."

Sara melted into Isherwood's arms, sobbing quietly against his chest. Isherwood turned to the people at the table. "How many bullets do we have left? Just give me your best guess."

"I've only got about 500-750 rounds left in Morganza split up between pistols and my .270. If I had more time, we could reload all the .22 casings. Give me the walkie, I'll tell Jim and Agnes to step up production asap."

"I'm thinking less than a thousand for the .22s, less than five hundred on the automatics," Patrick said looking at Justin.

Justin nodded in agreement. "But hey, Isherwood, I think we've barely touched the stockpile you had been hoarding for your pistols. We've been doing so much with the rifles that we haven't really touched the small arms ammunition."

"Maybe we could alter our strategy to pistol range somehow," Isherwood offered. "We probably have two thousand or more 9mm rounds."

The others recoiled at the idea, though Padre stayed thoughtful. "It's possible," he said. "We could use the raised roadway to our advantage. I-10 is like two or three stories higher than swamp level through there."

"Hey, maybe we've got a rifle that will chamber that 9mm luger ammo." Justin said, leaning forward. "Let's not give up on rifles yet. And we've found a lot of other toys in the armories besides, too."

"*And*," Patrick added. "We still haven't raided the police and sheriff's stations. There might even be another Wal-Mart on the way."

Isherwood was beginning to smile. "I think we've got the makings of a plan. Vanessa, can you radio a message back to them?"

Vanessa nodded. "Oh yeah, sure. Glenn said he'd come back on the radio at 5pm this afternoon."

Sara perked up at the sound. "Glenn?" she asked. "You spoke to dad?"

"Yeah, honey," Vanessa smiled. "And you will, too. After a while, okay?"

"Good, that's all really good," Isherwood said, standing up from the table. "Tell him to hold out. We're coming."

EPILOGUE: THE INTERSTATE

All the men, besides Monsignor and Jerry, had volunteered to undertake the rescue mission to Whiskey Bay. This meant the Three Amigos would be joined by Father Simeon and Marshall.

Isherwood didn't exactly feel comfortable with this following the kidnapping. He didn't know for sure if the bowling alley church and all its wackos had been completely wiped out. They had seen the zombies spill into the compound, but they hadn't actually confirmed any deaths or un-deaths. The driveway to the bowling alley had been filled with more cars than just the dirty sedan with the three crosses drawn through its dust. This made it more likely that it was their single base of operations, but there could still be others.

Tad had remained pretty tight-lipped about what she had seen inside the church, and Emma couldn't describe much coherently. Isherwood had demanded, however, that she say whether the church's pastor or leader was inside the building before she welcomed the zombies inside. He was, she admitted. "You don't need to worry about that bunch anymore, Isherwood." She had assured him before refusing to say anymore.

Fewer and fewer zombies seemed to be coming to the church fence, as well. Isherwood knew this could change at any time, but it made him feel less anxious about leaving. Vanessa also seemed to be adapting well to her and her son's new life at St. Mary's. She had taken Isherwood aside to tell him how thankful she was, not just for saving her, but for bringing her son back to her. She had been more than happy to take on additional duties besides monitoring the radio, especially when it came to protecting the children from kidnapping. "Not my son nor anyone else's are getting hurt under my watch," she had promised Isherwood. Seeing the flame in her eyes, he didn't question her commitment. She had even started, along with Sara, training the other women how to use the firearms. Even Aunt Lizzy was getting pretty deadly with a rifle – she'd even volunteered for bell tower duty. Isherwood mused that, if he did come back, he might be returning to an Amazonian kingdom of fierce female warriors.

All in all, Isherwood felt that the community would support itself despite the temporary loss of all the men. Though he may later regret it, he left them with a full stock of weapons and ammo. They would just need to find more ammunition along the way.

*****

Monsignor said Mass for the men before he would allow them to leave. When they eventually did leave, Old Blue was again at the head of their caravan. The caravan now numbered five vehicles. Isherwood had only begrudgingly added the National Guard vehicles to their caravan, when Uncle Jerry had promised he would modify the two CRVs as he had Old Blue. Father Simeon and Marshall were both able to drive either of the National Guard vehicles, the giant troop transport and the Humvee. Padre agreed to drive the Humvee and make up the caboose of the caravan.

The night before, not long after Vanessa broke the news of making contact with Whiskey Bay, they had started brainstorming about their ammunition shortage. They made first a list and then a map of the stops they would make before leaving town. The police and sheriff's stations would be first on the list. There were three or four stops to make just for these. Next, they brainstormed the houses where they would be likely to find ammo and possibly even more survivors.

Sara was especially helpful identifying who might have a stockpile of weapons and ammo in their homes, as these were precisely the same families that had joined her family out at Whiskey Bay in years past. Many were even family members, though nearly everybody in town was at least a cousin. The first name on the list was Brooks Moore.

*****

Whiskey Bay was an hour's drive from St. Maryville under pre-zombie conditions. The majority of Sara's family property lay directly south of Interstate 10, extending right up under the interstate which consisted mostly of bridges between Baton Rouge and Lafayette.

The raids they had undertaken along the way had been oddly fruitful. The police station, though otherwise destroyed in what appeared to be the officers' last stand, was a honey pot of 9mm ammunition. All of the police station's firearms, whether pistol or rifle, had been made for 9mm, as well. They thanked God for the chief's foresight, or whoever had made the decision to stick with the 9mm. Isherwood was especially grateful, as the score perfectly matched his own stockpile of ammo. The sheriff's office, however, had already been picked clean. The raids on the various residences had been fruitful, as well, if interrupted by burials – Brooks Moore's house was its own story.

After a full day and a half of preparations, side trips, and back roads, they caught sight of smoke still rising from the interstate. The caravan parked in the middle of a gravel roadway beside a cell phone tower. The vehicles formed a diamond pattern around the large Army transport truck they had liberated from the National Guard armory nearly a week ago. Old Blue parked out front, as always, while Isherwood's Jeep and Justin's Escalade parked on either side of the transport truck. Padre parked behind the transport in the Humvee.

Marshall got out of the transport and switched positions with Isherwood, getting into the Jeep. Isherwood closed the driver's side door and left the Jeep. He walked up to the gate of the chain-link fence that surrounded the base of the cell phone and radio tower. They were still about a mile north of I-10 and only slightly northeast of the camp where Glenn and the rest of Sara's family were trapped.

They were in the middle of the Sherburne Wildlife Management Area. *Just the right spot,* Isherwood thought to himself, *for a massive cell phone tower.* The tower was massive. Standing at the gate, Isherwood looked up at it, shielding his eyes from the bright sky. He had read on the various maps he'd managed to put together that the tower rose over 150 feet.

Isherwood left the gate and walked back over to the Jeep. He opened the back tailgate to retrieve the set of bolt cutters. "Padlock?" Justin asked from the turret of the Escalade.

"Yeah," Isherwood answered. "Thank God, too. I didn't want to be climbing over that razor wire."

"Yeah, buddy. It's up to you to repopulate the earth."

"You okay climbing that thing?" Padre asked.

Isherwood tried putting on a nonchalant ain't-no-thing face, but gave up. "Yup. Got to. We talked about it, and I'm the only one that has the slightest chance of recognizing the landmarks from up there. None of y'all have ever even been to the camp, except you, Justin, and that was only once. I'm not gonna lie – y'all better grab your umbrellas, because that's not gonna be rain that comes sprinkling down. It's gonna be my *pee.* My knees are already all wibbly-wobbily."

After about another half an hour, Isherwood clipped his harness to the ladder at over one hundred feet. He had climbed as high as his knees would let him. Even though he was tied off, he kept one gloved hand gripped tight to the ladder. He turned ever so slightly and caught a stiff wind. He flung his free hand back to the rung of the ladder. After a moment and a couple more "Hail Marys," he again let his left hand drop down. He slowly turned to face Interstate 10 at his back.

The interstate stretched for miles and miles, from horizon to horizon. He couldn't believe how high one hundred and fifty feet had taken him into the air. He felt like he could see clear to Texas on a clear day. Isherwood figured he must be five times as high as the St. Mary's bell tower. He was almost as high as the tops of the towers supporting the Audubon Bridge, which they had led the long snake of zombies across just over a week ago. *Had it been only a week?*

His stomach lurched as he thought about how high he was. He pushed the contents of his stomach back down and forced his swirling vision to clear. He dared not look directly down beyond his feet. What he saw stretching out behind him was enough.

Isherwood had thought he'd seen just about as many zombies as a person *could* see. He had been so wrong. From the crew he'd led across the bridge to Pickett's charge at the levee to, just a day or so ago, the swarm coming out of the spillway, he must have dealt with at least five thousand by now. But there were still so many more below him.

As he looked down now, he couldn't believe the wreckage contained in just one thin strip of roadway. Thin strands of smoke were rising diagonally into the sky from charred wrecks. After all this time, the smoke was still rising. Isherwood could even see flames still spilling out of cars along the roadway. He thought maybe one burned into the next, like a long fuse running all the way to Lafayette or Baton Rouge. The cities sat on either horizon. Thick smoke hung like black shrouds over both of them.

He was still quite a distance from the interstate. He squinted, but still couldn't see any sign of the undead. There was something odd about the roadway, though, like the hazy mirage that hangs around a gasoline fire. There was a strange sort of movement along the roadway. He put his binoculars up to his eyes, but he still couldn't make anything out except for the small lumps of cars – but wait. As his eyes adjusted, he began to understand what he was seeing.

It was like the videos he'd seen of the ocean floor, where endless fields of kelp or seagrass or whatever just drifted back and forth moved by unseen currents.

He could see the tops of the cars like flat squares, but not the sides.

The realization of what he was seeing struck him like a thunder bolt. The funny movement was them, moving listlessly side to side. They were just standing and waiting, some of them. Others seemed to be slowly groping their way toward one horizon or the other. Some seemed to be just drifting back and forth, as though first pulled toward the flames of Lafayette then slowly being distracted backward by Baton Rouge burning. Maybe it was the vibrations of explosions carried along the roadway that drew them first in one direction and then the other, alternating endlessly. They were completely filling the interstate like a slow-moving river pressing past and submerging the endless lines of cars and trucks like small islands in the stream.

He was not downwind of them, thankfully, nor even upwind, if that even mattered, but he could still hear the moans. They were not the excited moans that would rise from their rotting throats when living flesh was in sight. The moans were vast, however. It sounded like a giant, bored pipe organ made up of a thousand, thousand throats. It was horrifying, too.

Isherwood tried pulling his eyes away from the terrible scene. He eventually forced his eyes to scan the roadway up and down for exit ramps, especially directly behind him to the Whiskey Bay ramp. When he finally spotted it, he could see only the leading edge of it. But he could see enough. There was general, though still aimless, movement towards and leading down into the ramp. The river of zombies was narrowed there to thin rivulets where the cars were crammed too tight for zombies to pass abreast. No, it wasn't that the cars were crammed so much as − Isherwood blinked at the sight and felt his stomach lurch. Rotting flesh, scratched and torn from a thousand passing bodies was gradually damming up the exit ramp.

It didn't matter, though. Isherwood could see the zed heads spilling over the sides of the roadway. He couldn't see where they fell. The tree tops blocked that. He was pretty sure, though, that they just got right back up again.

Isherwood estimated that there were maybe two to three thousand per mile. *God, where had they all come from?* If they started shooting at any point along the roadway, they would merely break the dam at that point. The dead would eventually start raining down on them. It might only be a trickle at first as the dead slowly surged against maybe one hundred feet of roadway. They would eventually mound up, Isherwood imagined, against the sides of the roadway, maybe across the whole width of the road. The dead would start using the still-squirming mounds below them as a ramp. The river of dead would flow, then, up and over the sides of the roadway. The whole river would start spilling down over the sides of the road, right down on them.

He realized that Sara's family was lucky to be surrounded by *only* a few thousand. Any intrusion by their own rescue party would likely only add to these numbers. And by quite a lot.

"My God," he finally said to himself, lowering the binoculars. "What the *hell* are we gonna do?"

READ THE SEQUELS NEXT

The *Cajun Zombie Chronicles* continue in
Book Two
The Island Dead
- and -
Book Three
The Kingdom Dead

Check them out on Amazon, Kindle, and
www.holywaterbooks.com

Look for the following covers:

THE

ISLAND
DEAD

S.L. SMITH

THE
KINGDOM
DEAD

S. L. SMITH

About the Author
S. L. Smith

Scott Smith is an author, attorney, and theologian from Louisiana. Scott is a lover of all things Catholic: the Eucharist, the Blessed Mother, and especially the King of Kings, Who is the hidden connection between all history, Scripture, culture, and theology.

Check out more of his writing and courses below …

More from Scott Smith

Scott regularly contributes to his blog, The Scott Smith Blog at www.thescottsmithblog.com, WINNER of the 2018-2019 Fisher's Net Award for Best Catholic Blog:

FISHER'S NET AWARD
BEST CATHOLIC
BLOG 2018

— THE —
SCOTT SMITH BLOG
ALL ROADS LEAD TO ROME

AS SEEN ON ...
REGISTER
ChurchPOP
Aleteia
BIG PULPIT
New Advent
Catholic Online
SPIRIT DAILY
ALL SAINTS UNIVERSITY
CATHOLICISM.ORG

Scott's other books can be found at his publisher's, Holy Water Books, website, holywaterbooks.com, as well as on Amazon

His other books on theology and the Catholic faith include *The Catholic ManBook*, *Everything You Need to Know About Mary But Were Never Taught*, and *Blessed is He Who …* (Biographies of Blesseds). More on these below …

His fiction includes *The Seventh Word*, a pro-life horror novel, and the *Cajun Zombie Chronicles*, the Catholic version of the zombie apocalypse.

ALL SAINTS UNIVERSITY

EST. MMXVII

Scott has also produced courses on the Blessed Mother and Scripture for All Saints University.

Learn about the Blessed Mary from anywhere and learn to defend your mother! It includes over six hours of video plus a free copy of the next book … Enroll Now!

What You *Need* to Know About Mary But Were Never Taught

True Ghost Stories & Hauntings: Real Catholic Exorcisms

Truth is stranger than fiction … and scarier! This book contains accounts of *real* Catholic exorcisms. Many of these exorcism were made into movies, but even Hollywood with all its special effects and spinning heads couldn't recreate the true horror experienced by these possessed children.

These **true stories of exorcisms** are meant to inoculate you against the tricks and traps of evil. It is highly recommended that you read the Pray of St. Michael the Archangel (provided) before embarking on these accounts.

The real life accounts of possession that inspired *The Exorcist* movies and *The Exorcism of Emily Rose* are described in detail by the original eyewitnesses:

- The exorcism of Anneliese Michel, the heroic real-world Emily Rose
- Brandings and hideous faces appeared on the skin of "Roland Doe," whose exorcism inspired *The Exorcist* novel and movies
- The exorcism of Emma Schmidt, whose ridiculous outpouring of sludge inspired the infamous vomiting of *The Exorcist*
- And more, including the original texts of "Begone, Satan!" and the historic exorcism of Vervins, France

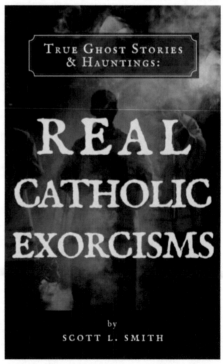

Beware! A common thread runs through all these stories. The evil unleashed in these possessions resulted from encounters with witchcraft, curses, and Ouija boards. Avoid these like your life and soul depends on it, because they do!

The proof is overwhelming! Possession and exorcism, as well as the devil, are real. Become sober, vigilant, and informed by reading this book.

St. Louis de Montfort's Total Consecration to Jesus through Mary

New, Day-by-Day, Easier-to-Read Translation

Popes and Saints have called this single greatest book of Marian spirituality ever written. In a newly translated day-by-day format, follow St. Louis de Montfort's classic work on the spiritual way to Jesus Christ though the Blessed Virgin Mary. Beloved by countless souls, this book sums up, not just the majesty of the Blessed Mother, but the entire Christian life. St. Louis de Montfort calls this the "short, easy, secure, and perfect" path to Christ. It is the way chosen by Jesus, Himself.

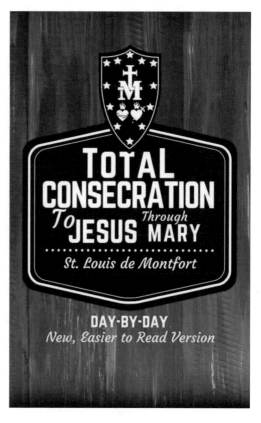

Pray the Rosary
with St. John Paul II

St. John Paul II said "the Rosary is my favorite prayer." So what could possibly make praying the Rosary even better? Praying the Rosary with St. John Paul II!

This book includes a reflection from John Paul II for every mystery of the Rosary. You will find John Paul II's biblical reflections on the twenty mysteries of the Rosary that provide practical insights to help you not only understand the twenty mysteries but also live them.

St. John Paul II said "The Rosary is my favorite prayer. Marvelous in its simplicity and its depth." He said "the Rosary is the storehouse of countless blessings." In this new book, he will help you dig even deeper into the treasures contained within the Rosary.

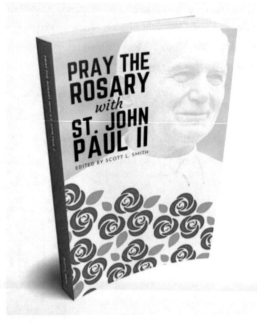

You will also learn St. John Paul II's spirituality of the Rosary: "To pray the Rosary is to hand over our burdens to the merciful hearts of Christ and His mother."

"The Rosary, though clearly Marian in character, is at heart a Christ-centered prayer. It has all the depth of the gospel message in its entirety. It is an echo of the prayer of Mary, her perennial Magnificat for the work of the redemptive Incarnation which began in her virginal womb."

Take the Rosary to a whole new level with St. John Paul the Great! St. John Paul II, *pray for us!*

What You Need to Know About Mary But Were Never Taught

Give a robust defense of the Blessed Mother using Scripture. Now, more than ever, every Catholic needs to learn how to defend their mother, the Blessed Mother. Because now, more than ever, the family is under attack and needs its Mother.

Discover the love story, hidden within the whole of Scripture, of the Father for his daughter, the Holy Spirit for his spouse, and the Son for his MOTHER.

This collection of essays and the All Saints University course made to accompany it will demonstrate through Scripture how the Immaculate Conception of Mary was prophesied in Genesis.

It will also show how the Virgin Mary is the New Eve, the New Ark, and the New Queen of Israel.

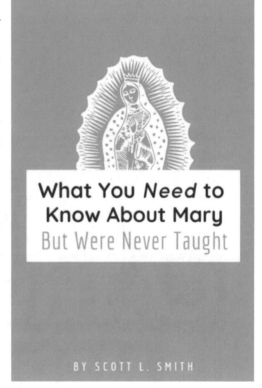

What You *Need* to Know About Mary
But Were Never Taught

BY SCOTT L. SMITH

Catholic Nerds Podcast

As you might have noticed, Scott is obviously well-credentialed as a nerd. Check out Scott's podcast: the Catholic Nerds Podcast on iTunes, Podbean, Google Play, and wherever good podcasts are found!

The Catholic ManBook

Do you want to reach Catholic Man LEVEL: EXPERT? *The Catholic ManBook* is your handbook to achieving Sainthood, manly Sainthood. Find the following resources inside, plus many others:

- Top Catholic Apps, Websites, and Blogs
- Everything you need to pray the Rosary
- The Most Effective Daily Prayers & Novenas, including the Emergency Novena
- Going to Confession and Eucharistic Adoration like a boss!
- Mastering the Catholic Liturgical Calendar

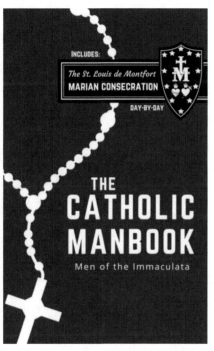

The Catholic ManBook contains the collective wisdom of The Men of the Immaculata, of saints, priests and laymen, fathers and sons, single and married. Holiness is at your fingertips. Get your copy today.

NEW! This year's edition also includes a revised and updated St. Louis de Montfort Marian consecration. Follow the prayers in a day-by-day format.

The Seventh Word

The FIRST Pro-Life Horror Novel!

Pro-Life hero, Abby Johnson, called it "legit scary … I don't like reading this as night! … It was good, it was so good … it was terrifying, but good."

The First Word came with Cain, who killed the first child of man. The Third Word was Pharaoh's instruction to the midwives. The Fifth Word was carried from Herod to Bethlehem. One of the Lost Words dwelt among the Aztecs and hungered after their children.

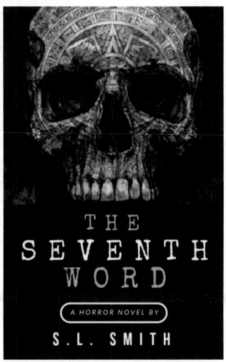

Evil hides behind starched white masks. The ancient Aztec demon now conducts his affairs in the sterile environment of corporate medical facilities. An insatiable hunger draws the demon to a sleepy Louisiana hamlet. There, it contracts the services of a young attorney, Jim David, whose unborn child is the ultimate object of the demon's designs. Monsignor, a mysterious priest of unknown age and origin, labors unseen to save the soul of a small town hidden deep within Louisiana's plantation country, nearly forgotten in a bend of the Mississippi River.

You'll be gripped from start to heart-stopping finish in this page-turning thriller from new author S.L. Smith.

With roots in Bram Stoker's Dracula, this horror novel reads like Stephen King's classic stories of towns being slowly devoured by an unseen evil and the people who unite against it.

The book is set in southern Louisiana, an area the author brings to life with compelling detail based on his local knowledge.

Blessed is He Who ...
Models of Catholic Manhood

You are the average of the five people you spend the most time with, so spend more time with the Saints! Here are several men that you need to get to know whatever your age or station in life. These short biographies will give you an insight into how to live better, however you're living.

From Kings to computer nerds, old married couples to single teenagers, these men gave us extraordinary examples of holiness:

- Pier Giorgio Frassati & Carlo Acutis – Here are two ex-traordinary **young men**, an athlete and a computer nerd, living on either side of the 20th Century
- Two men of royal stock, Francesco II and Archduke Eu-gen, lived lives of holiness despite all the world conspir-ing against them.
- There's also the **simple husband and father**, Blessed Luigi. Though he wasn't a king, he can help all of us treat the women in our lives as queens.

Blessed Is He Who ... Models of Catholic Manhood explores the lives of six men who found their greatness in Christ and His Bride, the Church. In six succinct chapters, the authors, noted historian Brian J. Costello and theologian and attorney Scott L. Smith, share with you the uncommon lives of exceptional men who will one day be numbered among the Saints of Heaven, men who can bring all of us closer to sainthood.

THANKS FOR READING!
TOTUS TUUS